GEOFFREY WILLS

Practical Guide
to
Antique Collecting

DRAWINGS BY A. J. TURVEY

GRAMERCY PUBLISHING COMPANY
New York

Library of Congress Catalog Card No.: 62-20296

This edition published by Gramercy
Publishing Company, a division of Crown
Publishers, Inc., by arrangement with
Arco Books, Inc.
C   D   E   F   G

Printed in The United States of America

Contents

Foreword

COLLECTING anything, antique or modern, is limited by two factors: the money available and the space to be filled. Having determined these basic essentials, it is then a personal matter. The taste of the collector may lead to watches or clocks, china teapots, or innumerable other things. The lucky acquisition of an admired piece may lead to a determination to get more of the same, or at least to find out what the admiration is all about.

This book is intended as a guide for the beginner, to help him through the bewildering maze of antique objects with which he is likely to come in contact. Also, it has much information to aid the more advanced collector. It sets out to help in identifying the age of a piece; to give clues that may reveal the actual maker, or at least his nationality; to indicate comparative rarity; and to suggest what is worth having and what to leave for others.

In a single slim book it is impossible to do more than outline some of the many antiques that may be met with ordinarily, and doubtless there are gaps. To try to fill them, some of the sections list a few selected books that will be helpful. It is well known that most books on art subjects are expensive, but those recommended costing around $5 and obtainable without much difficulty are marked with an asterisk (*).

The writer gratefully acknowledges help from the following: the Earl of Mount Edgcumbe for permission to photograph and reproduce the tapestry in Plate 8; Mr. A. L. Douch, B.A., Curator of the museum of the Royal Institution of Cornwall, for his co-operation when photographing pieces from the Edgar A. Rees, Hawkins, and other collections in the County Museum, Truro, shown in Plates 6, 10, 11, 13 and 17; Leicester Museums and Art Gallery for allowing reproduction of Plates 1, 2 and 3; the Metropolitan Museum of Art, New York City, for Plates 14, 15 and 16. Finally, he thanks his patient wife for reading and re-reading the proofs of the text.

Part I

FURNITURE

CHAPTER ONE

English furniture

WOODS

ABOUT fifty years ago, when the subject of English furniture first began to be studied and to be written about, it was divided conveniently into four distinct types. One writer called his books on the subject *The Age of Oak*, *The Age of Walnut*, *The Age of Mahogany* and *The Age of Satinwood*. It is not really quite as simple as that, for each of the so-called Ages overlaps the others and it is quite impossible to lay down strict dates as to when any one timber was introduced or when it finally, if ever, went out of favour. However, these clear-cut divisions do make it easier to deal with the subject, and it may be as well to keep to them; bearing in mind that the dates given are no more than very rough guides.

Oak is the traditionally English wood and while it alone was almost solely used for the making of furniture from the earliest times until about 1650, it has actually continued along with other woods right down to the present day. Old oak furniture is solidly made—the wood is very hard, and not only resists decay and woodworm but calls for time, patience and strength to fashion it—and many surviving pieces are of large size and noticeably weighty. At the time when it was popular, the houses of those who could afford furniture (other than plain and simple pieces) were large and the principal room, the hall, was quite often vast in size. Tables and cupboards were correspondingly

7

big, and to find a small and attractive piece of English oak furniture of sixteenth-century date today is thus not at all easy. The surviving specimens are eagerly sought and fetch high prices. Whereas a seventeenth-century chest may be bought for twenty pounds or so (on the whole, the larger the cheaper) a small cupboard of earlier date will cost several hundreds.

Oak furniture was made also on the mainland of Europe, and in appearance it is not unlike that made in England. Much was imported at the date it was made, and a further quantity of it was sent to London during the course of the nineteenth century.

As has been said above, oak continued in use for making furniture long after the wood had gone generally out of fashion. Pieces were made from it throughout the eighteenth and nineteenth centuries; pieces one would expect to find in walnut or mahogany which are discovered to be of oak. This was done mostly in the smaller country towns, where local craftsmen used timber that was available readily. While transport was both difficult and expensive, imported woods like walnut and mahogany would have been obtainable normally only near a seaport or a large town.

Walnut, an attractive light brown wood with distinctive dark patterns, came into use in the later years of the seventeenth century. Much of it was grown in England, but the imported French variety was usually preferred because it was better marked. The esteemed markings or figurings are to be found when a tree is cut across the base where the roots start to spread, and at the point (the crotch) where a branch springs from the main stem. The equally popular burr wood (marked with innumerable tiny dark curls) is found near burrs or lumps by clusters of knots.

Although a certain amount of furniture was made from walnut in the solid piece, it was used mainly in the form of a very thin sheet—veneer. This was glued down on to the main carcass of the piece; the carcass usually being constructed of pinewood (deal) or oak. The use of veneers enabled the craftsmen to select the best-marked portions and arrange them in patterns; a familiar form being known as 'quartering', where four successively cut rectangular pieces are laid on a surface so that their markings coincide evenly. Equally popular were 'oysters', circular pieces cut across a branch.

A severe winter in 1709 was responsible for the destruction of a great number of walnut trees in Europe, and was followed by the French prohibiting the export of the wood. To replace this source of supply, the American variety of the tree, which was already being sent to England in increasing quantities, was used instead. American walnut is not unlike European, and often cannot be distinguished from it. Some of it is quite free from markings, and this variety is often mistaken for mahogany when used in pieces of furniture made at the time mahogany was being introduced—about 1730–40.

The use of walnut declined quickly when the merits of mahogany were brought to notice, and it is rarely found in furniture made after 1740 until it came into fashion once more about a hundred years later. Then, it was used, as before, in the form of veneers on cabinets, tables and other pieces, and in the solid for chairs. These latter have come into rapidly increasing favour during the past fifteen years, and while pre-1939 they could be bought for a matter of a few dollars a set, will now cost something nearer $100 for six.

Walnut furniture of the late seventeenth and early eighteenth centuries is not easy to find. Veneered pieces were extremely popular in the late 1920's and fetched high prices. This fact proved an irresistible temptation to a large number of skilful cabinet-makers, who attempted to make the supply meet the demand and poured out large quantities of fakes of varying merit. The best of them are very difficult to detect; the poorest were so badly made (in a vain attempt to make them look as though they had suffered 200 or more years of handling) that they have mostly fallen to pieces. Apart from making fakes entirely from new timber, much ingenuity was exercised in making them from bits of old furniture that were then worthless. This deception calls for a lot of knowledge to detect it. Walnut furniture must be bought with caution, and, preferably, from a trusted source.

At one time Queen Anne walnut furniture was very popular
in the United States, but it was soon found that central-heated
rooms caused glue to dry up and veneer to fall off in an alarming
manner. Consequently, veneered furniture is no longer looked
on with affection in America.

Mahogany is such a well-known timber that it is scarcely
necessary to say much about it in the way of description. To
most people it is a familiar reddish-brown wood, and it has been
used for making furniture since about 1730. The timber was
imported from the Bahamas, from San Domingo, from Cuba,
and from Honduras. Strictly speaking these different places
produced trees that were not usually true mahogany, but the use
of the word spread to cover all timbers of a red-brown colour
that resembled it closely in appearance and could be worked in a
similar manner.

It is the Cuban variety that has the very distinctive markings
beloved of cabinet-makers in the second half of the eighteenth
century. This variety was used often in the form of veneers, as
was walnut, in order to show the light and shade of the figurings
to the best advantage.

Mahogany is very strong, seasons quickly and does not tend
to warp and split, is seldom attacked by woodworm, and is a
good timber to work. It could be obtained in large enough pieces
to make large table-tops without joining, which had not been
possible before, and not only does it take a pleasing smooth
finish but is excellent for carving. It is therefore not hard to under-
stand why, once it had been introduced, it quickly became popular
and stayed for long the principal timber used in cabinet-making.

Satinwood came from the West and East Indies, and was in use
for furniture-making from about 1780 until 1810. It is a wood
with a warm yellow colour, and has a close grain that takes a
high polish. It was used mainly as a veneer, but unless handled
carefully by the cabinet-maker it has a tendency to split. Towards
1800 it was used in the solid for making chairs and for the legs
of veneered tables. Satinwood was an expensive timber, and it was
used, on the whole, only for special pieces for wealthy clients.

Satinwood furniture was sometimes elaborately inlaid with other light-coloured woods, but mostly it was decorated by having oil-painting as part of the design. Much of it is said to have been the work of the woman artist, Angelica Kauffmann, but this is seldom, if ever, true. Chairs, as well as tables and cabinets, were decorated with painting, and this took the form of small bouquets of flowers and garlands of trailing leaves which suited the slender shaping of the woodwork.

About 1900 there was a revival of interest in eighteenth-century satinwood furniture. Old pieces were brought out from cellars and attics, where they had been hidden as unfashionable, and were restored and sold for large sums. At the same time, a large number of copies and near-copies were made for those who could not afford the real thing. These pieces have now had half a century of wear and tear, so the prospective buyer should be on his guard. Often, too, the old painting on an eighteenth-century piece has been removed because it was worn, or for some other reason, and has been replaced by the work of a modern artist. This happens commonly with table-tops, which inevitably get scratched and stained in daily use. Such restored pieces are worth less than those on which the decoration is original.

Other woods

While oak, walnut, mahogany and satinwood are recognized by most people, and one or more of them is present in almost every home, there are a large number of other woods used by cabinet-makers in the past that are not so easily identified. To describe them in words so that they can be named positively is not possible, but a general indication of their appearance and uses may be helpful.

Amboyna. A wood from the West Indies with a distinctive burr, looking like closely curled hairs over the light brown surface. It was used in the form of veneer.

Cedar. The harder varieties of this wood, known as Red Cedar, were used for making the linings of drawers in some better-quality eighteenth- and nineteenth-century furniture. It is not to be confused with the spongy open-grained cedar used for making cigar-boxes, which it resembles in sharing the same pleasant smell.

Ebony. A black wood of very close grain and heavy in weight, which was popular for veneering at the end of the seventeenth century. Later, it was used in inlay and especially for the dark lines in stringing.

Elm. Somewhat similar in appearance to oak, this wood was in use during the seventeenth century and later. It is as hard as oak, but it tends to twist with age and is susceptible to woodworm.

Harewood. The veneer of the sycamore, stained a grey colour, was called 'harewood' in the eighteenth century. It has pleasing rippled markings, and was popular both as a veneer or for use in inlaying.

Lignum vitae. A hard, heavy West Indian wood, of a dark brown colour with black markings. It was used occasionally as a veneer, but was principally made into bowls and cups, and similar pieces.

Maple. The American 'bird's eye' maple has small markings all over its yellow-brown surface, and was popular during the nineteenth century. It was used particularly for veneering picture frames, but is found also on furniture.

Rosewood. An East Indian wood with a close grain and distinctive blackish lines on a brown ground. Although it was in use during the eighteenth century, it became widely popular during the nineteenth both as a veneer and in the solid when it was imported also from Brazil. It is a heavy timber, and chairs made from it are often found to have been broken from their own weight when carried.

Yew. The familiar tree of English churchyards makes a wood of a medium brown colour used sometimes in the solid and also for veneers. Furniture using either type is much sought after, and when found is usually expensive.

Papier mâché. This material, an imitation of wood, was made in England from the second half of the eighteenth century. The more usual method of making it was to stick layers of paper together and leave them to dry, either flat or in moulds. The article was rubbed down until smooth and then painted several times and decorated; each layer of paint was baked gently in an oven to harden the coat and produce the final high gloss. Trays and tea-caddies were among the earliest articles made from papier mâché, but during the nineteenth century small tables, chairs and even bedsteads, were also produced.

FORMS OF DECORATION

Carving

The earliest way of decorating a wood article was perhaps by means of carving. In the case of oak, the hardness of the timber severely limited the craftsman, but the coming of walnut was more encouraging. It lent itself to the chisel readily, and in some instances the carving was decorated additionally with gilding to give a very rich effect. Pieces treated in this manner, partly polished wood and partly gilt, are known as 'parcel-gilt'. Mahogany was the carver's delight, and he was able to show with it all his skill. In addition, fretting was applied sometimes to mahogany pieces. This took two forms: the wood was pierced in a pattern with a fine saw, or the effect of a thin pierced sheet stuck down on the surface was imitated by carving. This latter type is known as 'semi-fret', and is often to be seen in Chippendale's designs.

One other wood must receive a mention: pine. This was in use from the end of the seventeenth century, and its texture provided an excellent medium for carving. In most instances this was concealed under gilding or paint, and almost all the elaborately carved mirror-frames and tables of the eighteenth century will be found to have been made from this timber.

Silver and gold

Towards the end of the seventeenth century a certain amount of furniture was made of which all or most of the surface was covered with embossed sheets of silver. A famous suite of this description, consisting of mirror-frame, candlestands and a table is at Windsor Castle; there is another at Knole, Kent, and yet another was sold by auction in 1928 for no less than 10,100 guineas. At about the same period, in imitation of gold, pieces of furniture were painted with successive thin coatings of a plaster composition called 'gesso' (pronounced 'jesso'), carved in what appear like embossed patterns, and then spread with gold leaf. Later, in the eighteenth century, the gesso was painted on carving and followed the design of the woodwork itself. Tables, and even chairs, were treated with gilding, but the most popular furnishings to be decorated in this manner were mirror-frames. The gold leaf, pure gold beaten into small flat sheets thinner than tissue-paper, was made to stick to the plaster surface by means of a type of gum or by oil-size. The former, which needs greater preparation of the groundwork is called 'water-gilding', and can be highly polished afterwards; the other, 'oil-gilding', is a simpler method and the work cannot be burnished.

Inlay

At the same time as carving came into use, there was intro-duced an alternative type of decoration: inlay. This took many different forms over the years, varying from simple straight lines in wood of contrasting colour to the ground (called 'string-ing'), to the elaboration of marquetry in which the inlay often covers a greater proportion of the surface than the ground. This latter was in great demand shortly before 1700, when the form known as 'seaweed marquetry', so complicated in pattern that the walnut ground could scarcely be seen at all, came into prominence. This fashion did not last for long after the start of the new century, but there was a revival of it in a weak manner in about 1860. Many different woods were used in marquetry; some were dyed in bright colours and others darkened by scorch-ing to enhance the effect. Pieces of bone, tortoiseshell and mother-of-pearl were also used sometimes.

A popular inlay on walnut furniture is known as 'herringbone', and consists of a band of two narrow strips of the same wood placed together with their grain meeting diagonally. The effect accounts for the name, which is alternatively 'feather-banding'.

A further type of inlay is known as 'cross-banding'. It consists of a band of inlaid wood, often to be found at the edges of a table-top, in which the grain of the wood runs outwards.

Inlaying with a narrow strip of brass was done occasionally in the eighteenth century, but mostly in Regency times when

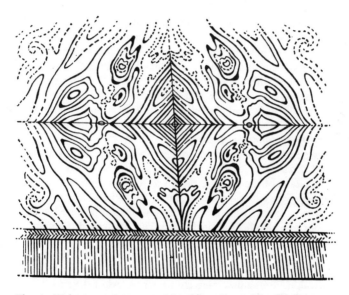

Fig. 1. Walnut veneers quartered, with a line of herring-bone or 'feather banding', and cross-banding at the bottom.

more ambitious shapes, such as stars, were attempted also. It was very popular, and is looked on now as a feature of the period.

Mouldings

Mouldings varied in shape with each period, and their study will help to identify the date of a piece of furniture. The narrow half-round moulding found on the edges of many eighteenth-century drawers is known as 'cock-beading'.

Lacquer

Lacquering was practised in the Far East for many centuries before it was introduced into Europe. Chinese and Japanese craftsmen decorated furniture by painting it carefully with many coatings of the sap of a locally grown tree, then after it had been well smoothed it was painted with designs in gold and colours. Some of this work was brought to England at the end of the seventeenth century, and became popular enough to be imitated as closely as possible by both professional and amateur artists, and much furniture made in England in the early 1700's was ornamented with this pseudo-oriental lacquer. In addition, pieces of English furniture were sent out to the East to be embellished in the authentic manner by local craftsmen, and quantities of cabinets and other furnishings of Far Eastern manufacture were sent to all countries of Europe.

In addition to the lacquer just described, in which the smoothed surface was painted upon, often with small areas raised to emphasize details of the pattern, there was another type in which the designs were cut and then coloured. The finished article showed a smooth black panel into which were incised coloured designs about one eighth of an inch deep. This was called 'Bantam' or 'Coromandel' lacquer, and was made often in the form of large folding screens. Some of them were of as many as twelve leaves, each about two feet wide and eight feet high. Occasionally, on arrival in Europe they were cut up regardless of their pattern to make cabinets or other pieces of furniture.

Although the principal interest in lacquered furniture was at the beginning of the eighteenth century, it remained fashionable throughout the Georgian period and pieces were made at all dates. A considerable quantity of plain old furniture was lacquered in the 1920's when there was a revived fashion for it. Chairs and tables, tea-caddies and trays, made both of wood and of papier-mâché, were painted with a black lacquer and inlaid with mother-of-pearl and then gilt during the 1850's. Some of these pieces were also painted with attractive panels in oil-colours.

Black is the most common ground colour of lacquer, but

pieces in which the ground is red, blue, green, yellow, or white, are known. The two last named are the rarest and the most valuable.

Polish

The finish applied to antique furniture when it was made was to rub it down with fine abrasives until it was as smooth as possible, apply linseed oil or a mixture of beeswax and turpentine and continue to rub until the desired gloss was produced. This made a hard-wearing surface, especially when the process was continued occasionally in the home. About 1820, came the process known as 'french polishing', in which a shellac varnish is applied to the furniture by means of a 'rubber' made of linen wrapped round cotton-wool. A french-polished surface is not as hard-wearing as the original method, it is damaged easily, but is much easier to apply and quickly came into general use. In the course of time, most old furniture has been repolished by this more modern method, and it is very rare indeed to find an untouched piece with its original surface.

STYLES

TUDOR: Elizabeth I to James I (1558–1603)

Oak was in use for furniture during the reigns of the Tudors, and for most of the seventeenth century as well. It is a heavy and strong wood, which grew plentifully in England but was imported also, and the furniture made from it is both weighty and durable. Being a hard wood it is not easy to carve, although it can be decorated with inlay. On the whole, the hardness of oak determined the styles in which it was made and ornamented, and in spite of the difficulty of working the timber surprisingly elaborate carving and inlay was carried out. Construction was simple: the mortice and tenon joint held fast with a wooden peg, or dowel. The most noticeable feature in design is the exaggerated bulbous turned leg on tables, bedstead posts, and supports on the fronts of cupboards.

JACOBEAN: James I to Cromwell (1603–1649)

Walnut began to be used, but in the solid and then only occasionally. As this wood is prone to attack by woodworm, a great amount of it was probably destroyed and it may have been much more popular than we know. The bulbous support, so popular earlier, is seldom seen and is replaced by simpler turning.

CROMWELLIAN: Oliver and Richard Cromwell (1649–1660)

Oak and walnut remained the principal woods, but the most common feature is again the use of turned ornament. Fronts of chests were decorated with turned columns cut into two halves lengthwise, and inlaid with simple patterns in mother-of-pearl, bone or ivory. Turning on chair and table legs was often in a series of knobs, known as 'bobbin-turning'. Seats of chairs were sometimes of leather, fixed with large brass-headed nails.

CAROLEAN: Charles II to Flight of James II (1660–1689)

After the years of austerity under Cromwell and the Puritans, the accession of Charles II was the signal for an outburst of luxury and extravagance; according to some, never surpassed. Walnut superseded oak, although the latter continued in use on a diminished scale as it does even now. Veneers and marquetry, lacquer and embossed silver were introduced for the decoration of furniture, and the use of mirrors on the walls of rooms became general. The tall-backed chair, known earlier in a simple pattern, became the object of attention from turners and carvers and is the typical feature of the period. The back and the front rails were elaborately carved, the design often centring on a pair of cherubs holding a crown aloft, and the seat and back panels were caned.

WILLIAM AND MARY (1689–1702)

This was a period that saw the arrival of large numbers of Dutch workers, who came over from Holland, with King William III, who was also Prince of Orange. Having been born and brought up in Holland, it is not unexpected that both he and his Queen (daughter of James II of England) should be more fond of the productions of that country than those of England. To these monarchs is owed the creation of a problem for twentieth-century collectors in trying to distinguish some of the Dutch furniture from English. Also, as the reign was only a short one, it is not easy to tell William and Mary furniture from Queen Anne; pieces with showy decoration are said usually to have been made before 1700. Cabinets and chests often had a plain turned ball-shaped foot (replaced in more recent times by a bracket foot of later design) and turned legs favoured the inverted cup. Stretchers (cross-pieces connecting the legs of chairs and tables) were of a 'wavy' shape and usually had a turned pointed knob (finial) where the two pieces crossed over.

QUEEN ANNE (1702–1714)

Walnut furniture is always associated with the name of this Queen, and some of the finest surviving pieces date from her time. Marquetry was seldom used, and every effort was made to show off the grain of walnut veneers to the best advantage on pieces of simple outline. Lacquer remained popular. The cabriole leg was the most important introduction, and was often carved with a shell on the fat curved knee. Mirrors were more plentiful and of smaller size, and upholstery with both silks and needlework became general.

EARLY GEORGIAN (1714–1730/40)

Much furniture similar to that of Queen Anne's reign was made. At the same time, gilding became popular and was used for mirror-frames, tables and even chairs. The Kent or Palladian style was fashionable, and this showed architectural features (Wm. Kent, whose name is given to the style, was a prominent architect) such as the broken pediment, and a frequent use of marble tops for tables.

MID-GEORGIAN: Chippendale (1730/40–1770)

The introduction of mahogany followed a brief period in which red walnut (from Virginia) replaced the familiar French walnut.

At first, mahogany was used in the same styles as walnut pieces had followed, but before long the superior working qualities of mahogany led to new designs. Many different styles were collected and adapted by Thomas Chippendale, a cabinet-maker, who published them in his book, *The Director*, in 1754. Thus almost all furniture made between about 1750 and 1780 is known today, conveniently, as 'Chippendale':

French 'Chippendale' features curved outlines, and particularly the cabriole leg with an outwardly curling toe.

Gothic 'Chippendale' shows the arch with a pointed top (lancet-shaped), as a part of the design for doors of bookcases, in the form of piercing for the backs of chairs, and in fretting on legs.

Chinese 'Chippendale' uses Chinese pagodas, Chinese figures and birds and other Far-Eastern forms. One or other can be found on all pieces of furniture of this type, but the mirror-frame often has them all.

LATER GEORGIAN: Adam, Hepplewhite and Sheraton (1770–1810)

A number of styles succeeded and partially overlapped each other during these years:

Adam: the Adam brothers, Robert and James, were primarily architects, but their interest in design did not stop with the building itself. Not only did they plan the layout of their mansions, but usually they decided the decoration and colouring of the principal rooms and the furniture to go in them. Their work was inspired by ancient Greek and Roman art, and most of their decorative ideas were borrowed from those sources. The honey-suckle (anthemion), the ram's head and hoof, and garlands of husks are typical features. The work of the Adams was carried out between 1760 and 1790 and many of their designs for furniture were actually made by Thomas Chippendale's firm.

Hepplewhite: George Hepplewhite was a cabinet-maker whose business was run later by his widow, who published a book of his designs. These show pieces of simple form and small size; one of the most noticeable is perhaps the chair with a heart-shaped or a shield-shaped back. Sometimes the shield holds a pierced and carved Prince-of-Wales feather.

Sheraton: Thomas Sheraton published his first book of patterns in 1791. His designs show furniture that is much more slender in line than hitherto, and he led a return to the use of inlay; with this his name seems to be linked inseparably. Inlay often took the form of cross-banding and stringing, and a common feature was an oval shell of satinwood, scorched to imitate shading. After about 1800, square legs were replaced by turned ones with reeding. Sheraton's most characteristic chairs have rectangular backs with horizontal bars. Use was made of satinwood, as well as the more general mahogany, either painted or inlaid or left quite plain.

REGENCY (1800–1820)

The Regency style is a combination of at least three, or any one may be found alone in a piece made during the period. The three principal styles are:

Greek and Roman: figures of mythological gods and goddesses, the lyre (used as the shape of table-ends), the lion's-paw foot.

Egyptian: sphinxes, Egyptian heads and feet as tops and bases of columns; crocodiles.

Chinese: Chinese patterns, shapes and colours; of which the contents of the Pavilion at Brighton are outstanding examples.

All types of unusual woods were used, as well as mahogany, and there was frequent use of brass for inlay and gilt bronze for mounts. Chairs were smaller in size than in earlier periods, which explains why they are so very popular today. Early Regency chairs had legs shaped like a curved sword (the sabre, after which they are named), but later they were turned.

WILLIAM IV AND EARLY VICTORIAN (1820–1840)

Much of this furniture can be confused with that made earlier in the Regency period. Although many of the designs are similar, they were carried out in a much heavier manner, and chairs, tables and other pieces are coarser and clumsier in appearance. The sabre leg was no longer used, and almost all furniture had turned supports, often tapered and carved.

MAKERS AND DESIGNERS

The majority of English cabinet-makers are known to us only by their names; only rarely is it possible to say who made a particular piece. When this can be done it is for one of two reasons: either because the original bill has been preserved, or because the name of the maker was inlaid, stamped or printed on a paper label inside the article. The following are some brief notes on a very few of the more important designers and makers who worked in the eighteenth century.

Samuel Bennett. A London maker who was working at the beginning of the eighteenth century. A cabinet is known with his printed label in one of the drawers. Also, there are three cabinets in existence which have his name inlaid on the inside of a door.

William Kent (1686 to 1748). An architect, and about the first in England who not only designed a mansion but also some of its contents. His furniture is heavy in appearance and bears much carving, and as his tables and chairs were usually gilt the effect is very rich.

Thomas Chippendale (1718 to 1779). The best known of all English cabinet-makers and designers. Born at Otley, Yorkshire, he came to London and eventually opened a workshop in St Martin's Lane. His book of designs, *The Gentleman and Cabinet Maker's Director*, was published first in 1752, enlarged in 1762, and is the most famous of its kind in any country. Chippendale's own firm made pieces for many of the biggest mansions in England, and some of it remains in the rooms in which it was first placed, and for which it was designed. On his death, his business was carried on by his son, also named Thomas.

John Cobb (died in 1778) and **William Vile** (died in 1767). Cobb is recorded as being notorious for a very haughty manner, and stories are told of the difficulties into which this led him.

Some of his furniture has been identified, but his partnership with William Vile is equally responsible for his importance. Together they were cabinet-makers to George III, and pieces they are known to have made are among the finest of the eighteenth century. Some of their work for the Royal Family is still at Buckingham Palace. William Vile died in 1767, but his partner seems not to have been in favour for no further goods were supplied to the King and Queen after that year.

William Ince and **John Mayhew** (working between 1760 and 1810). These cabinet-makers, who had a workshop in Soho, London, published a pattern book in 1763. The book contains about three hundred designs for different types of furniture in the Chippendale manner, but only a few pieces are known that were made by the firm.

George Seddon (1727 to 1801). The biggest cabinet-making business in London in the eighteenth century was conducted by George Seddon in Aldersgate Street, where he is said to have employed four hundred workmen. Some of the furniture made there has been identified from the bills that were preserved with it.

George Hepplewhite (died in 1786). George Hepplewhite's name is on a book of designs issued by his widow in 1788, but little else is known about him.

Gillow's. The firm of Gillow had workshops at Lancaster, Lancashire, and were prominent cabinet-makers during most of the eighteenth century. They had a showroom in Oxford Street, London (later the site of Waring and Gillow's showroom), and sent their finished goods south by sea. Late in the century they sometimes used a metal stamp with their name to mark their pieces, and are the only English firm known to have used this French method of marking before about 1820.

Thomas Sheraton (1751 to 1806). Little is known of the history of Thomas Sheraton. He was born at Stockton-on-Tees, Durham, and came to London. His famous book of designs, *The Cabinet Maker and Upholsterer's Drawing Book*, was published in four parts between 1791 and 1794, and his *Cabinet Dictionary* in 1803.

Although he was trained to the trade as a youth, he is not known to have practised as a cabinet-maker.

William Moore (working between 1780 and 1815). After some years at work in London, Moore opened a business in Dublin, where he specialized in inlaid furniture in the Sheraton style. Much other furniture was made in Ireland during the eighteenth century, but it is often indistinguishable from its English counterpart. Mahogany tables on especially slim cabriole legs are considered usually to be of Irish make, but much research on this subject remains to be done.

CHAPTER TWO

Dictionary of English pieces

Barometers. The barometer was invented and came into use during the seventeenth century and until the introduction of the modern 'Aneroid' type it consisted of a tube of mercury standing in a cup of the same metal. The pressure of the atmosphere on the surface of the mercury in the cup caused it to vary in height in the tube, and the level could be read off against a scale. Alternatively, the rise and fall could be shown on a circular dial and indicated by a movable pointer. The earliest barometers were made by the eminent clockmakers of the day, were often enclosed in cases of walnut and are very rare and valuable. In the later eighteenth century many were made in mahogany cases and included a thermometer and a damp-detector (hygrometer). These are not hard to find, and their price varies today according to condition and whether or not they are in working order.

Beds. In the past, people spent more money on their beds than on any other article of furniture. The wood framework which was usually of four-poster type, was only a part of the expense, the majority of the time, labour and money going on the elaborate hangings which enclosed it and kept the occupant warm and draught-free. The oldest to survive in any numbers is the Elizabethan carved four-poster, with its elaborate headboard and carved roof (tester), and of these the best known is the Great Bed of Ware. This was mentioned by Shakespeare in *Twelfth Night*, and has found a final home in the Victoria and Albert Museum, London. Mahogany beds were made in much the same form as oak ones had been, although taller and more graceful in appearance, and it was not until 1850 that the four-poster went out of fashion and the brass bedstead took its place.

Buckets. Buckets made of mahogany bound with brass and with brass handles were made from about 1760. They were used to carry plates to and from kitchen and dining-room, and have a

25

long vertical opening from rim to base so that the plates could be removed easily. Rare examples were made with flat sides decorated with fretwork. Brass-bound buckets without the vertical opening are described as *Peat Buckets.*

Bureaus. A bureau is a form of writing desk, and has a number of names: including escritoire, scriptor and secretaire. The earliest type, dating from about 1675, was a cabinet on an open stand, with a hinged front that let down to make a writing surface. Shortly after that date came a similar piece, but with the top sloping instead of upright. Later again, drawers were used in place of the stand, and the pattern that is still made came into being. Many sloping-top bureaus were made in the form known as a *bureau-bookcase*; that is, with a bookcase above the bureau.

Another variety is in the form of a straight-fronted chest, the front of the upper dummy drawer (or upper two drawers) hinged and falling to reveal a writing-space with pigeon-holes and smaller drawers. This type is called generally a *secretaire.*

Bureaus and secretaires, with or without upper bookcases, were made in one form or another from about 1700 onwards, and not only in walnut and mahogany but also lacquered. It is important to make sure that a bureau- or secretaire-bookcase remains as it was made, and has not been 'married' subsequently. Often, a straightforward bureau has had a bookcase, more or less fitting and matching, placed on it and the value falsely increased.

Butler's Trays. A large oblong tray on a folding X-shaped stand, usually of mahogany, was used by the butler as an extra and movable sideboard. Late eighteenth-century examples are of various types: plain, brass-bound at the corners, and with all four sides of the tray hinged to fall flat. Another type has the rimless top hinged across the centre and in one with the base, and the whole article folds up. These are sometimes known as 'coaching tables'.

Cabinets. Cabinets with hinged doors, with or without drawers inside, were made in the later seventeenth century, and much attention was paid to their decoration. They were veneered with rare woods, inlaid with marquetry and embellished with plates of embossed silver. They were placed on stands of turned wood, and later on elaborately carved giltwood bases. Many lacquered cabinets were imported from the Far East, and placed on similar stands for use in English rooms.

Cabinets on stands did not retain their great popularity in the eighteenth century, but their place was taken by book and china cases with glazed doors. About 1800 low cabinets standing on the ground came into fashion, and many of these had marble tops and the doors were inset with panels of silk or with gilt brass trellis.

Caddies. The caddy owes its name to a Chinese weight, a *catty* or *kati*, which equals about one and a third pounds. Much of the tea coming from the East was doubtless packed in amounts of one catty, and the name of the quantity became corrupted into that of the box to hold it. Although tea-caddies were made from different materials, many were of wood and it is proper therefore to mention them under the heading of Furniture. Few, if any, survive from before about 1740, but in 1752 Chippendale showed in his *Director* designs for a number of them, elaborately shaped and carved. Each succeeding designer influenced the shape, colouring and ornament of the tea-caddy, and the immense number of variations in pattern are too numerous to list. Many of them had silver containers inside a wooden outer case, others had removable wooden boxes. In the nineteenth century it was common to fit them with two boxes, one each for green and black tea, and a glass bowl; the latter described variously as for holding sugar and for blending the teas.

Canterbury. This is the name given to a low open stand with divisions, a drawer beneath and short legs, for holding music. They were made in mahogany from about 1800, and later in rosewood and walnut. No one knows how they got their name, but it is assumed that one was designed in the first instance for an Archbishop of Canterbury. They are very popular nowadays, not always for holding sheet music but for newspapers.

Card Tables. Playing-cards were introduced into England in the fifteenth century, and doubtless a special table for use with them followed shortly. None survive before walnut ones made in the reign of William and Mary, with the typical folding tops lined with needlework or cloth. They are rare, but later examples in mahogany survive in large numbers. Almost all are lined with cloth, and many have the inside corners recessed to hold candlesticks; others have oval sunken spaces to hold counters or coins. Late in the eighteenth century card tables were often made in pairs, and examples are found occasionally veneered in satinwood and of half-round shape.

After 1800 they were made on a pillar support with splayed legs and brass-capped toes.

Chairs. Before about 1500 chairs were a rarity, few homes had even one, and most people sat on benches, stools or chests. The chair, when one was to be found, was reserved for the use of royalty and the most noble. By the time of Henry VIII and Elizabeth I, armchairs of various types had begun to be made in quantity, and quite a number survive now. They are made of oak, with a straight or nearly straight back, with turned legs and curved arms, ornamented with carving or inlay. They have plain wood seats, and were used with the aid of a cushion.

Single chairs (those without arms) were probably made at an earlier date, but being less strongly constructed, few have survived that were made before about 1600. Most are quite plain, with the upper part of the back and the seat covered in silk or embroidery. As the seventeenth century progressed, and walnut or painted beechwood replaced oak, a number of fresh styles came and went. Turning, either in the form of bobbins or barley-twist was popular, and the use of caning instead of upholstery was introduced from the Far East. Finally, came the fashion of tall-backed chairs, heavily ornamented with turning and carving, with seat and back caned. Many of these were imported from France and Holland, where a similar fashion reigned, and it is a matter of argument as to where many of these chairs actually originated.

Gradually, caning lost favour, and its place was taken by elaborate upholstery in velvet or figured silk, but in either case with deep-fringed and coloured edgings. Although many of the single chairs were upholstered on both seat and back, others—still with the high back—featured a tall carved and pierced back panel and the first use of cabriole legs. By 1715 the cabriole leg was in general use, and the back of the chair had started to become square in shape: no longer was it the characteristic tall and narrow feature of the previous century. The centre of the back, called the 'splat' was usually a panel of solid or veneered wood and of shaped outline, and the top of the back was rounded. Most chairs showed some carving, especially in the form of the claw and ball foot. Some very finely carved chairs have feet in the shape of lions' paws, with lions' heads on the knees; others have arms which finish in heads of eagles.

By 1740, with the coming of mahogany, the use of carving on chairs was widespread, the back continued to get lower until it was more or less square, and the cabriole leg remained popular. The top of the back was usually of a cupid's bow shape, the seat nearly square and often of generous size. Probably the most famous English chairs are those for which Chippendale shows designs in his book, *The Director*, where they are called 'ribband back chairs'. These have the back carved and pierced in an intricate pattern of ribbons with a central bow. A number of these masterpieces have survived the wear and tear of two hundred years.

The last quarter of the eighteenth century saw a further number of different fashions come and go. Robert Adam designed chairs, many of them with oval backs, shaped seats and turned legs, and in carved and gilt wood; an integral part of the decoration and furnishing of the room for which they were created. His suites often ran to a dozen armchairs, with large settees and stools, all covered in tapestry or figured silk. With other designers, backs varied greatly; shield, heart, round, or square, were among the shapes used. Towards 1800 came a fashion for beechwood chairs, many with shield-shaped backs, painted in colours with flowers and other subjects. At about this date, too, satinwood chairs were made, and these also were painted.

In the earlier years of the nineteenth century, chair backs were almost all nearly square, and the legs were curved forward—the 'sabre' shape. Mahogany chairs of this type, much smaller in size than those made in the years before, are very popular today, the most decorative, eagerly sought and, therefore, the most expensive, being those inlaid with brass lines. Rosewood was also a wood used for chair-making at this time, but it was imitated closely in painted beech.

Hall chairs were made during the eighteenth century and later. They were more for display than for comfort, with wood seats, and the backs were usually painted with the coat-of-arms or crest of the owner.

The *Windsor chair* was first made in the eighteenth century, and is still being turned out in large numbers. The arched back and shaped wood seat appear much the same in chairs of 1760 as in those made two hundred years later. They owe their popularity to their strength and lightness, and to the fact that they can be made cheaply. About 1770 they cost five or six shillings apiece, but they are dearer now.

Chests. The chest is agreed to be the most ancient form of furniture, and surviving examples go back in date to the thirteenth and fourteenth centuries. Many of these extremely old ones are simple in design, and bear very little in the way of ornament. Others, however, are carved liberally, with strong iron bands to protect the contents from thieves. As long ago as 1166, Henry II commanded that a chest should be put in every church to collect money for fighting the Crusades, and that each should be fitted with three locks; each lock should be different, and each key held by a separate official. In 1278 a similar order related to the safe keeping of church books and vestments. In the same way, chests were used in houses for the storage of clothing and other property.

The early chests are seldom seen outside churches and museums, but later ones, dating from 1650 or thereabouts, are much less rare. Usually they are made of oak, the front and lid divided into recessed panels, and decorated with carving or inlay or both. By the end of the seventeenth century few were being made, and their place was taken by more complicated and useful pieces such as chests of drawers and cabinets. Occasionally, in the eighteenth century, chests of mahogany and of giltwood were made, but not in large numbers. Today chests are much less popular than they once were; partly because of the inconvenience of a piece of furniture with a lifting top.

Chests of Drawers. The chest of drawers was evolved from the simple chest, noted above. Drawers were added underneath the chest, and before very long the entire piece of furniture became the casing fitted with drawers as we know it today. The earliest were made about 1650, of oak, inlaid, and later with the fashion for walnut they became very popular in that wood. Many were decorated with marquetry and with lacquer, and plain walnut examples were veneered to show the grain of the wood at its best. About 1720, small chests of drawers, called for no recorded reason 'bachelor's chests', were made, these have tops that fold over and rest on bearers that pull out from the body of the piece. Being no more than about thirty inches high, two feet in width and a foot from back to front, it is no wonder they are much in demand and very expensive. When old walnut furniture was enjoying a vogue in the 1920's examples of it were dear and labour cheap; many fakes were made. Now, forty years later, some of these have had a lot of wear and tear, and careful examination is needed to distinguish between old and new.

Chests of drawers continued in popularity throughout the eighteenth century, and very fine examples were made in mahogany. Some were of serpentine shape, the top drawer fitted as a dressing table with divisions for combs, brushes and toilet accessories, and with the front corners heavily carved. Simpler ones were of straight outline, and relied on gilt metal handles for their ornament.

Inlaid mahogany chests of drawers came into fashion about 1780, and were made with straight or bowed fronts. They

continued to be made with slight variations in design for many
years more.

Chiffonier. A small bookcase or cupboard with an upper part
of open shelves. A decorative piece of furniture that was first
made about 1800, and continued to be popular throughout the
nineteenth century.

Coasters. Wine-coasters are stands for bottles or decanters for
use at the dining-table. Some took the form of wooden trays with
rims, others were of japanned papier-mâché, silver or plate.
Cheese coasters were usually made of mahogany and date from
about 1790. They are boat-shaped with a square base raised on
small casters. Today, they are rarely used to hold the large round
cheeses for which they were designed, but have a fresh lease of
life as fruit containers.

Coffee Tables. While any small and low table can be, and is,
called a coffee table, the term is applied particularly to the sets
of three or four tables made from about 1790; of which the latter
were called 'quartetto tables'. As their name implies, they
were made in sets of four, and were so designed that each
slid into the other. When so placed they took up no more
room than the largest. Made in mahogany and in rosewood, they
have been in production almost continuously and old sets are
scarce.

Commode. This is a French word describing a type of chest of
drawers made in that country. In England, it was applied in the
eighteenth century to pieces of furniture designed in the style of
Louis XV or Louis XVI, and fitted with drawers or with doors
to form a cupboard. Such pieces were highly decorated with
carving, marquetry, lacquer or inlay, and would have had pride
of place in the most important room of a house.

Console Tables. Tables made for fixing against a wall and having
no legs at the back. They came into fashion early in the eighteenth
century, and were made often in pairs.

Cradles. These small beds for children were usually made to
swing; achieved either by mounting them on rockers, or suspend-
ing them in a framework. Early ones of oak are rare, but eigh-

teenth-century specimens made of mahogany are sometimes to be seen.

Cupboards and Wardrobes. Cupboards for the storage of clothes and linen were made from the fifteenth century onwards; until the late seventeenth century they were usually of oak and with the doors divided into panels. They are rare, as are the walnut ones made about 1700. Mahogany cupboards and wardrobes are more plentiful, but being large in size they are not greatly in demand for use in the smaller rooms of present-day homes. The eighteenth-century wardrobe often had the upper part with sliding shelves enclosed within doors, and the lower part with drawers. In this form it is called today a *Gentleman's Wardrobe*, and in many instances the insides of the drawers and the upper shelves have been removed to make hanging-space for clothes. In the later years of the century, the mahogany cupboards were inlaid, and others were veneered with satinwood or made of pine and painted.

Court cupboards of oak were made in the sixteenth and seventeenth centuries. They consist of open shelves with supports at the corners; the front ones carved. *Hall* or *livery cupboards* were made during the same years, and have doors to the upper and lower parts. For many years there has been confusion between court and livery cupboards, but at the moment of writing the above descriptions are the accepted ones.

Corner cupboards of three-cornered shape and with flat or bowed fronts, were made in the eighteenth century. They exist in oak, walnut, mahogany and pine; the latter painted or lacquered. Many are decorated with inlay, but rare specimens have carved and gilt ornament.

Davenports. First made at the end of the eighteenth century, the davenport is a small desk. It has a sloping-top which is hinged, and a series of drawers down one side. They were made in both rosewood and mahogany; early examples have short square legs, later ones are turned.

Desks. Like the davenport, above, a desk is a piece of furniture with a sloping-top for writing. Sixteenth- and seventeenth-

century examples were small, portable sloping-top boxes which
would contain pen, ink and paper and provide for their use.
Some early eighteenth-century examples were fitted with stands,
but in Victorian times the original box-type returned to favour.
These latter were of mahogany or rosewood and bound with
brass. Nowadays the term desk is applied to almost any piece of
furniture at which writing can be done, including what was once
called a writing table. These have a leather-covered top and tiers
of drawers below, often with a central knee-hole recess for comfort. Large, double-sided versions of this type are called *partner's
desks*.

Dining Tables. The first dining tables of which survivors remain
are the type known as *refectory tables*. They are made usually of
oak, and one of the earliest, at Penshurst Place in Kent, has a
typical thick top of joined planks supported on three separate
trestles. Later, came a lower part in one piece with heavy legs
united by stretchers at their bases and rails at the tops. The
Elizabethan dining table, also of oak and constructed in this
manner, was often carved and inlaid, the legs being turned into
strikingly large bulbous swellings. An alternative type at this
period was the *draw table*, which extended by means of leaves
at either end sliding in and out from below the principal top.

Refectory tables stayed in use throughout most of the seventeenth century, but towards 1680 came large circular tables on
gate-leg supports. Many of these are four feet or more in diameter,
and it seems probable that their use was for dining.

Mahogany dining tables survive in large numbers, and are of
many types. Early ones, of about 1740, have falling side-flaps
supported by swinging outwards the hinged legs; others are in
sections and become as many as four separate tables when taken
apart. Late in the eighteenth century came the type with each
section supported on a central pillar with splayed legs and brass-
capped toes; a type that is very popular today for the practical
reason that the legs are out of the way of the diners.

Dressers. A piece of furniture on which china or silver was
displayed. In the seventeenth century it was a long table with

drawers, usually raised on legs, and made generally of oak. In the eighteenth century came the fashion of fitting a superstructure of shelves, sometimes with small cupboards at either end, and these are often called *Welsh dressers*. Rare examples are made of yew wood.

Dumb Waiters. A set of revolving trays of different sizes supported on a central pillar, and used beside the dining table. Eighteenth-century mahogany examples had circular trays and tripod bases, some nineteenth-century rosewood ones were oblong and had four-legged supports.

Foot Stools. These came into use at the end of the eighteenth century, and continued to be popular from then onwards. The upholstered tops were often covered in needlework.

Gate-leg Tables. These tables, which have the distinctive feature of a gate-like hinged leg to support the top flap, have been made continuously in one form or another from at least the seventeenth century until today. The earliest were made of oak and are rare, but those of the middle and later years of the seventeenth century can be found sometimes. They vary in size from a large dining table some seven feet in length to small tea tables about three feet in diameter. In most instances the supports are turned. Somewhat similar tables were made also of walnut, but these are scarce. Small mahogany gate-leg tables are often of a type known as 'spider leg', because of their thin supports. Many gate-leg tables were made in Victorian times, when this method of construction was very popular.

Gout Stools. Stools that have adjustment to raise or lower their tops were made from about 1790 for the relief of sufferers from gout. Another pattern, of 'X'-shaped construction, with thick padding, was made at about the same date.

Knife Boxes. Cases, with hinged lids, for holding knives, spoons and forks, were made of wood or of wood covered in shagreen (fish skin). Although existing from the middle of the seventeenth century, most of the surviving examples are of eighteenth-century date and made of inlaid mahogany. The most popular type had a sloping top and serpentine-shaped front, but others in the form of a vase on a foot are sometimes seen. Some of the latter were made from satinwood, inlaid or painted.

Lanterns. We do not usually think of a hall-lantern as a piece of furniture, but Chippendale has designs for them in his *Director*, and one made to his pattern is in the Philadelphia Museum of Art. Old wood ones are very rare, but gilt metal examples, especially of Adam design, are to be seen. Many of them date from long after the eighteenth century.

Mirrors. The first mirrors to be used in England were flat plates of highly polished metal—called 'steel', but actually an alloy of copper and tin—they were of small size and very heavy. Venice had a monopoly of making mirror-glass, and it was exported from there to the rest of Europe. In the seventeenth century Venetian workers began to make it in England, and the use of glass mirrors for personal use and for decoration became widespread.

At first they were framed in a similar manner to paintings, and it is difficult to decide whether a seventeenth-century frame was made for a picture or a mirror. Those known as 'cushion-shaped', with a deep rounded edge, veneered with walnut, carved, inlaid with marquetry or lacquered, were among the earliest made.

By the end of the century, very large mirrors had become fashionable. There was a limit to the size of a sheet of glass that could then be made, so a frame was filled sometimes with more than one sheet, and often bordered with a number of smaller ones. The mantelpiece in the principal room of a mansion would have a large mirror over it, and these *overmantel mirrors* were sometimes framed in walnut and gilt wood; the frame also incorporating an oil painting and filling the entire space above the fireplace. Overmantel mirrors continued to be made, and their styles followed those of wall mirrors down the years.

During the reigns of Queen Anne and George I, many small mirror-frames were made, and these were veneered with walnut sometimes enriched with gilt carving. Many of them survive today, but the greater proportion of so-called Queen Anne mirrors are little more than thirty years old.

Gilding continued in fashion, and mirrors appeared in frames of pinewood brightly gilt and carved flatly in gesso—a type of plaster composition which could be carved and smoothed and took the gold-leaf in a satisfactory manner. By 1735–40 taste had changed once more, and large mirrors of severe design with tall rectangular glasses were appearing on fashionable walls.

Mirror frames were the object of great attention from carvers and gilders throughout the eighteenth century; the most elaborate examples of their work came in the middle years. Then, fashion allowed them to incorporate what they pleased on the frame: shepherds and shepherdesses, Chinese gods, waterfalls, sea-shells, ruined temples and bouquets of flowers vie for attention on some of the extreme examples, which are masterpieces of the carver's art. Following these exuberances, came the more restrained style set by the Adam brothers. Frames were then often oval in shape, and embellished with honeysuckle, husks and winged seated griffins. At the end of the eighteenth century, the frame was even more plain, and the most popular ones had the glass flanked by a column at either side, and sometimes with a painting on glass at the top.

Although it had been known for many hundreds of years, the circular convex mirror was not widely popular until early in the nineteenth century, when many examples were made. Most of them had a moulding of ebony surrounding the glass, a deeply moulded gilt frame decorated with gilt balls, and an eagle with outstretched wings at the top. The eagle often holds a chain with a gilt ball at the end of it, and many of the mirrors have arms for holding candles, the best examples fitted with hanging cut-glass drops.

Small mirrors on stands for use on the dressing table—*toilet mirrors*—were framed in silver, and often with needlework. Those supported on uprights and a base fitted with drawers were introduced about 1700. Many were veneered with walnut, or lacquered. Mahogany examples, of late eighteenth-century date, are often inlaid and fitted with oval or shield-shaped mirrors. In about 1800, the mirror became oblong in shape, horizontal instead of upright, due to changing fashions in hairdressing, and the uprights supporting it were turned instead of square or moulded.

About 1790, *cheval mirrors*, large dressing mirrors on movable stands with casters, came into use. Most of them have frames of mahogany, but sometimes they are of rosewood or satinwood.

Pembroke Tables. These have folding flaps, which can be supported on hinged concealed brackets at each of the longer sides of the rectangular top. The legs of the earlier ones are square and tapered, but by about 1790 they change to round ones with turned ornament. They came into use about 1750, and are said to owe their name to a Countess of Pembroke who first ordered one. The Pembroke table was made in mahogany, satinwood, and sometimes harewood, and decorated with inlay and painting; frequently they show workmanship of the highest quality.

Pier Tables. Tables made for placing against the piers of a room: the areas of wall between windows. Originally they had mirrors above them. They are sometimes called *side tables*.

Screens. These have two purposes; to keep away draughts from doors and windows, and to ward off the heat of a fire. Draught screens were first imported at the end of the seventeenth century from China, and they are made of lacquered wood with designs in gold and colours, or with the designs incised (*Bantam* or *Coromandel Lacquer*). Many are of eight or ten folding panels, and they stand up to eight or more feet in height. Screens of similar folding type, but not quite so large, were made with panels of painted or embossed leather.

Fire screens are small and portable, and date also from the late seventeenth century. The stands were of all styles, following the fashion of the time when they were made, and the screen itself often held a panel of tapestry or needlework.

Settees and Sofas. A settee is understood to mean a chair with space for more than one person to sit, and a sofa is a larger piece of furniture with room on it to recline. Neither of the terms seems to have come into general use until the early eighteenth century, but some settees with tall backs in the form of two chair-backs joined together date from about 1680. Shortly, they became very fashionable, and elaborately carved and heavily upholstered examples were made. Most of them reveal considerably more fabric and trimming than they do woodwork. In about 1730 there came a reversion to the first style, and the settee appeared again like an armchair but having the back in duplicate or triplicate, side by side. This type continued to be made throughout the eighteenth century, but the upholstered variety was made as well; each conforming in outline and detail to the fashion of the time when it was produced.

The *love seat* is a very narrow settee or sofa with only just sufficient space for two persons to sit on it; hence its name. Many early eighteenth-century armchairs were widened ruthlessly into love seats about thirty-five years ago, when the demand for them greatly exceeded the supply.

Settles. A settle is a bench with arms and a back. Many of them had seats that were hinged to reveal lockers. They date back to the fourteenth and fifteenth centuries, but most surviving examples are of seventeenth-century make and are usually of oak. By about 1700 they were being made on legs and without lockers beneath the seats, and cannot be distinguished from settees.

Sideboards and Sidetables. The dresser, mentioned earlier, before it was fitted with shelves, was a sidetable. Early in the eighteeenth century these were highly carved and often gilt, had no drawers, and were topped with a slab of coloured or white marble. By 1760, they were of mahogany with a top of the same timber, and Chippendale prints designs for several of this type. It was Robert Adam who added a pair of pedestals, one at either end of the table, but it was nearly 1780 before the sideboard was given drawers and became the article recognized today. One of the drawers was usually fitted with divisions lined with lead or zinc to hold wine-bottles. Until about 1800 they were supported on square tapered legs, but later these were turned. Great care was lavished by their makers on sideboards, and the choicest figured woods were chosen for veneering and inlay.

In the first quarter of the nineteenth century a further modification in design took place, and the sideboard comprised a pair of pedestals with a single drawer between, but unlike the earlier Adam type these were in one piece.

Sofa Tables. A sofa table is not unlike a Pembroke table, having similar folding flaps which are hinged and can be raised and held by concealed brackets. The flaps are, however, at the narrow ends of the top, and the supports of the table vary in design; they are never straight, as in the Pembroke. Those with supports in the form of a lyre are the most esteemed. The sofa table came into use about 1800, many were made of rare woods and were highly finished, and good examples fetch high prices.

Stands. A number of types of stands were made at all periods, and they include *candle and lamp stands* and *urn stands*. The first were made in pairs or sets, and varied in height from three to four feet. The urn stand was a small table on which a tea-urn was placed when tea was taken; tea being expensive and teapots therefore of small size, the latter needed refilling frequently. Thus, a kettle on a stand with a spirit-lamp beneath was a part of the tea service during the eighteenth century, and a small table on which it could stand was made for the purpose. Most have four legs, there is a low gallery or rim round the top, and a slide on which the teapot could rest while being filled. Circular-topped small tables on tripod bases were perhaps made for the same purpose, but nowadays are usually called *wine tables*.

Steps. Portable sets of steps were made in the eighteenth century for use in libraries. Many were ingeniously designed to fold away and be transformed into a table, others became a chair. Steps were made also for the purpose of climbing into a bed.

Stools. Stools are shown in illuminated manuscripts dating back to the twelfth century, but none survive that are older than about 1500. Those of the seventeenth century are the oldest usually to be met with outside museums and stately homes, and are of the simple pattern called *coffin stools*, or more recently, *joint stools*. They are supported on turned legs which splay outwards slightly and are united by plain stretchers, the tops usually having a moulded edge. The majority are of oak, and their sturdy dowelled construction has kept them intact for three centuries.

With the Carolean tall-back chairs came stools with carving to match the cresting and legs of the chair, and upholstery that replaced the hard wooden seat used previously.

Most of the stools made in the eighteenth century, whether in walnut or mahogany, follow the styles in fashion for chairs: from the cabriole leg with ball-and-claw or lion's-paw foot to the variety seen in Chippendale's *Director*.

In past years stools have received attention from furniture fakers, and many have been made from chairs; equally, the process has been reversed and stools have been transformed on occasion into chairs. The underneath framework will usually show what has happened if it is given a very thorough examination.

Tea Tables. Portable tables for holding tea-ware came into use with the introduction of the beverage late in the seventeenth century. The most familiar are the circular-topped mahogany examples made between 1740 and 1780, supported on tripod bases. These were often carved elaborately, and some had tops with shaped and moulded edges, known as 'pie-crust' from the slight resemblance they bear to that pastry. Tables of folding-top card-table type, but with the insides of the tops polished were used also for serving tea.

Trays. Eighteenth-century wooden serving trays were made in mahogany and other woods; inlaid oval examples in the Sheraton style replacing mahogany ones with pierced or brass-bound rims.

What-nots. Square tiers of open shelves, four or five in number, with corner supports and, usually, a drawer in the base, used for holding ornaments or books, etc. They were made principally in mahogany or rosewood from about 1800.

Wine-Coolers and Cellarets. A wine-cooler is a receptacle for cooling wine, a cellaret for storing a few bottles of it. The essential difference is that a cellaret usually has a cover and the cooler has not. They both came into use about 1730, and were made of mahogany with a lead lining. Some were inlaid elaborately or mounted in cast gilt metal, but the majority were bound with plain bands of brass.

Window Seats. Towards the end of the eighteenth century there was a fashion for wide stools with upturned ends, and these were then called *window stools*. Designs for them are shown by Hepplewhite in 1788, and they were made in mahogany and in gilt wood.

Work Tables. A small table with a hinged top concealing spaces for sewing accessories, which was introduced late in the eighteenth century. Many have a silk-covered hanging bag, and the top is sometimes inlaid with squares for chess. Many were elaborately made and highly finished with painting and inlay.

Writing Tables. There is confusion between writing tables and desks, but the latter are generally those with tiers of drawers to the ground, whereas a writing table is on tall legs. These were made throughout the eighteenth century, but became more popular towards the end of the period. About 1790, the *Carlton House* type was introduced; this has rounded ends at the back with low tiers of drawers facing the writer. Not a great number would seem to have been made, and surviving old examples are very rare. Mostly they are of mahogany, but a few are known in satinwood. Copies have been made since about 1900, and these may deceive the unwary.

CHAPTER THREE

Continental furniture

FURNITURE made on the mainland of Europe varied from country to country, but both craftsmen and ideas were interchanged from time to time. Local tastes and the use of local timbers often played a part in creating a fashion that spread eventually from east to west. There is no space here to deal with the detailed history of the subject in each individual land, but some general notes may be helpful. French furniture, having attained a world-wide interest and importance, is described at greater length.

FRANCE

French furniture of the sixteenth and seventeenth centuries is not greatly different from that made elsewhere in Europe at those dates. However, the principal wood used in England was oak, but in France it was walnut which was plentiful there. Just as many foreign workers came to London, so did others to Paris; it is almost impossible to distinguish an Italian-made cabinet from one made in France by an Italian craftsman. It was not until the end of the seventeenth century that French furniture gained its recognizable distinction. The first to give his name to a style there was André Charles Boulle (1642–1732), who perfected a marquetry, originating in Italy, employing tortoiseshell and brass which was used mostly on furniture veneered with ebony. This is known now either as Boulle or Buhl work, and the majority of it that has survived was made in Victorian times, or later. Old work of the eighteenth century is very valuable ($3,000 to $6,000 for a piece would not be considered extraordinary), but the nineteenth-century copies fetch a tenth or so of this.

Louis XV

This monarch has his name coupled with the most extravagant of furniture designs, known as Rococo; a style that spread throughout Europe. The term means ornamented with shells and scrollwork and similar patterns, and until one grows accustomed to it, the dictionary definition of 'tastelessly florid or ornate' may often be thought to apply. To our eyes it is noticeable principally for a generous use of curved lines, and an

Fig. 2. Louis XV armchair.

'unbalanced' look. Out of its elaborate setting there is no doubt that Louis XV furniture appears very showy, but when it is seen in the rooms for which it was designed it takes its place unobtrusively in the decorative scheme.

The French had a liking during the eighteenth century for small tables and cabinets, chests of drawers (called *commodes*), large writing tables with leather-covered tops having a row of drawers beneath and tall legs, and upright cabinets with drop-down fronts concealing a writing space. Veneering was the usual decoration, aided by parquetry and marquetry set off with ormolu mountings. When compared with the sophisticated outside appearance, most of the pieces exhibit very rough finishing

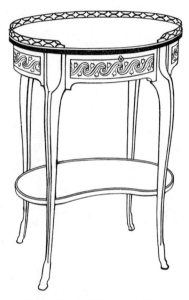

Fig. 3. Louis XV small table.

of the woodwork not usually seen, and a glance at the inside or underneath of a piece will prove this.

Many of the small tables and cabinets are supported on delicately curved cabriole legs so slight that it is a wonder they can stand without breaking. Chests of drawers always have a slab of coloured marble as the top, and many other pieces are similarly finished. Chairs and settees were carved usually of beechwood, sometimes finished with gilding and sometimes painted in pale colours. Mirror-frames were gilt, and are often very like English ones of the same date.

46   ANTIQUES

Louis XVI

A style that coincided roughly with the reign of this king: 1774 to 1793, and that is associated with a predominance of straight lines in place of curves. Tables and cabinets usually had square instead of rounded corners, and legs were square or

Fig. 4. Louis XVI armchair.

rounded in place of cabriole. Furniture continued to be veneered and fitted with ormolu mounts, and many pieces were decorated with plaques of Sèvres porcelain; some of it in blue and white to imitate Wedgwood ware. There was a revival of interest in Boulle work, more of this was made to fill the demand, and it can be distinguished only with difficulty from that made earlier. Chairs no longer had the cabriole leg, but usually oval backs and turned legs; in both this and the preceding period they were often upholstered in tapestry.

Empire

Following the luxurious tastes of the eighteenth century, there was a revival of comparative austerity when the excesses of the Revolution finally died away. Instead of the richly mounted and colourful marquetry, the fashion was for plain mahogany

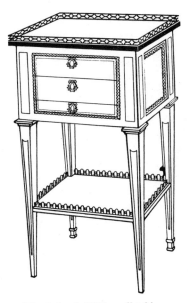

Fig. 5. Louis XVI small table.

with perhaps an inlay of brass and restrained ormolu mounts. The mahogany used was often of a darker colour and more even grain than that favoured in England, but there are a number of similarities between the Empire style in France and the Regency. Chairs, in particular, often had the sabre leg in both countries.

It must be emphasized that old French furniture was costly when it was made, and has always maintained a high price.

During the past hundred years, those who could not afford
the genuine article bought copies which were made to sell at
reasonable prices and, apart from these copies which were not
made with intent to deceive, it has paid the unscrupulous to
spend time and money in making fakes. Remembering the years
that have passed since most of it was made, some two centuries,
and the fact that much was destroyed and damaged during the
Revolution, it is surprising that so many fine examples have
survived. A lot of these have been repaired skilfully: lost veneer
replaced, lost tops of tables restored, cupboards converted into
drawers, and so forth. Thus, with French furniture as much as
with any other, the collector must be very cautious indeed, and
the subject needs careful study before its qualities can be appreciated and assessed.

With English furniture it is rarely possible to name the maker
unless bills or other definite evidence has been preserved. Only
very occasionally is a cabinet-maker's label found pasted inside
a piece. French craftsmen, however, had the custom of marking
their productions (or the majority of them) with a steel stamp
bearing their name or initials. This was followed, when applic-
able, by a monogram of the letters J M E, standing for *jurande
des menuisiers-ébénistes*; showing that the article was up to the
standard required by the Corporation of French cabinet-makers
and had been inspected by their appointed jury. This custom, also,
has had the attention of the fakers, and more pieces bear the
alleged stamp of famous craftsmen than they could ever have had
the time to make.

The following is a very brief list of the more eminent French
cabinet-makers of the eighteenth century, of whom there were
nearly 1,000 working in 1790:

J. H. Reisener	L. Boudin
Bernard Van Reisen Burgh (Stamped B.V.R.B.)	P. Roussel
J. F. Oeben	D. Rontgen
Martin Carlin	C. C. Saunier

Roger Vandercruse Lacroix   A. Weisweiler
(Stamped R.V.L.C.)
G. Jacob
(Specialized in making chairs)

GERMANY

At the time when Queen Anne walnut-veneered furniture was being made in England, rather similar pieces were made in parts of Germany. They can be distinguished from one another by the more extravagant lines of those from Germany: whereas an English chest might have a gently shaped front with straight sides, the German equivalent would have a deeply curved front, and the sides would be curved also. German walnut bureau-bookcases (a sloping-front bureau with a cupboard above) have been offered from time to time as genuinely of English manufacture, and in some instances their more obvious curves have been skilfully reduced. Later in the eighteenth century Germany copied the prevailing French styles.

HOLLAND

Dutch furniture has always had close links with English, and much Dutch and Flemish oak has been, and still is, mistaken for English work. In the times of William and Mary and Queen Anne, there was a flow of Dutch craftsmen to England, and much of the furniture of those periods could have been made in either country. Some of the walnut-veneered and marquetry pieces are, like the German, rather over-shaped and too heavily decorated to be of English make.

Large two-door cupboards of walnut and ebony were popular, these were constructed to take to pieces for transport and are found in Holland and farther afield. Dutch chairs of a design reminiscent of the work of Robert Adam, with carved ornament of leaves and ribbons, were made in mahogany and can be mistaken for English.

Towards the end of the eighteenth century, the Dutch cabinet-makers made some attractive furniture of oak veneered with satinwood and inset with shaped panels of lacquer. Tables, cabinets and fall-front secretaires are to be found in this style.

Much of the Dutch walnut and mahogany furniture inlaid with marquetry of flowers and birds, often bookcases with glazed doors, and sloping-front bureaus, have had the marquetry added long after they were made. This was done when plain furniture was temporarily unfashionable.

ITALY

Italian furniture inspired or followed the design of most of the main types of other European countries. Marquetry was first used there, and developed later in Holland and England, and by Boulle in France. The furniture of Italy varies from district to district, not only in details of design but in the timber from which it was made. Many pieces were veneered, others were gilded, and others lacquered. The painted or lacquered furniture made in Venice in the eighteenth century is much in demand at present.

SCANDINAVIA

Much English furniture was imported into the Scandinavian countries in the eighteenth century. The most famous and valuable that was actually made there was the work of a Swede, George Haupt (1741 to 1784), trained in Paris and London, who made furniture in Stockholm in the Louis XVI style. His work is rare and valuable.

CHAPTER FOUR

American furniture

VERY little American furniture is to be seen outside the United States, and the majority of English and Continental museums, large and small, show none whatsoever. The reader (U.S. or British) may be interested to know how it differs from the European. Occasionally, pieces are found in English homes, whence they may have been brought back by returned settlers, and if offered by auction it is found they fetch high prices in comparison with similar English articles. This higher valuation is justified by the fact that old American furniture is rarer than English, much of it is already in museums in the United States, and there is a large number of keen collectors to compete for every piece.

Seventeenth-century American furniture resembles that made in England some fifty years earlier, and this lag in time continued to be present through most of the eighteenth century. However, by 1800 or so, with improved conditions in the new country and better shipping facilities across the Atlantic, there was very little difference between the interior of a fashionable mansion in New York and one in London. As the early settlers in New England were from the British Isles it would be expected that the furniture they made was like that of their homeland as they remembered it. So it was, but local variations occurred very soon. For instance, the tall cane-backed Jacobean chair was copied continually in America and remained popular throughout the eighteenth century, but instead of the back being filled with a panel of caning often it was given a series of shaped uprights and became the 'banister-back' chair.

Similarly, when mahogany became fashionable, English-style straight-fronted kneehole desks and chests were made in Newport, Rhode Island, with what is termed a 'block front'; a type of break-front of serpentine shape, with one or more of the flat 'blocks' carved with a sunray or shell. Such variations on the designs from London became popular in the locality where they were made, but they did not spread far. The various districts that had been colonized each had their speciality, but the most notable was certainly the furniture made in Philadelphia. Basically of mid-eighteenth-century English design, these chests, tables, chairs and other pieces were ornamented with carving and fretwork in a style that differentiates them clearly from London work.

Later, in the first half of the nineteenth century, an American version of Sheraton furniture was very popular. The most famous examples were the work of Duncan Phyfe, who had emigrated from Scotland, and whose name is probably the best known of that of any American cabinet-maker. Born in 1768, he died in 1854.

Apart from pieces made in the cities, American collectors eagerly seek old country-made furniture, and there is great interest in Windsor chairs and similar pieces which resemble closely their European originals. Eighteenth-century German settlers in eastern Pennsylvania made versions of their home furnishing— known as 'Pennsylvania German' or 'Pennsylvania Dutch'— mainly in light-coloured fruit woods, and these also are very popular in the United States.

One noticeable difference in cabinet-making on both sides of the Atlantic is in the timbers that were used. Much furniture was made in America from local woods: such as apple, cherry, and maple. Walnut remained in use in some districts long after mahogany had become fashionable elsewhere, and in Pennsylvania it was the principal wood until about 1850. Thus, one finds a piece of American furniture in a recognizable rendering of the Chippendale style, but instead of being made from mahogany, as would be expected, it is in walnut, or even cherry wood.

Certain pieces of furniture are named differently in America from what they are in England. Four of the most important are:

Lowboy: a modern word describing what is called in England a dressing table; a low table fitted with drawers and raised on legs.

Highboy: a lowboy with, in addition, a chest of drawers on top.

Bureau: described in England as a chest of drawers: the English bureau or writing desk is known in America as a 'slant-front desk'.

Secretary: called in England a bureau-bookcase: a sloping-front writing desk with a bookcase above it.

In addition to Duncan Phyfe, mentioned above, other important cabinet-makers are:

William Savery, of Philadelphia (1721 to 1787).

John Townsend and his brother-in-law, **John Goddard,** of Newport, Rhode Island (both lived about 1730 to 1785).

John Cogswell, of Boston (about 1769 to 1818).

CHAPTER FIVE

Points to look for in telling old from new

General appearance

The general look of a piece of furniture tells the expert whether it is old or not, but this is a matter of experience. If you are interested in old furniture see as many genuine pieces as you can; go to museums where you are certain of the authenticity of the articles. Slowly the eye and mind can be trained to recognize whether the appearance of a piece is true or not.

Colouring

The ageing of wood alters its colour according to the timber from which it is made, and according to the treatment it has received over the years. Even the hidden inside parts change with time; if a drawer-lining is scraped it will show at once how the surface has aged. Equally, the old polished outside surfaces mellow, and repolishing changes the colour of the wood completely.

Construction

It is worth while studying the methods of making furniture, and how they have changed from time to time. How, for instance, the crude dovetails on the heavy drawer sides of 1600 were modified and improved in the course of the century. When examining a piece of furniture in a strong light, it is as well to look for signs of alteration, and to try to reason what was done and why. New screws differ markedly from old; prior to about 1850 they did not taper to a point. Also, the slot in the head was hand-cut and seldom central; in modern machine-made screws it is invariably exactly across the middle of the head. Veneering has been mentioned on earlier pages when it came into use with the introduction of walnut. It may be added that old veneers were cut with a saw by hand, and are consequently quite thick; many of them almost an eighth of an inch. Modern veneers, however, are cut with a machine-driven saw, and are much thinner. This, with other factors, is a useful indication of the genuineness of a piece. The use of some of the rarer woods implies that an article cost more for materials and probably also for labour, and that it was probably made to a high standard throughout. The better-quality eighteenth-century pieces were fitted with oak linings to the drawers, but in exceptional instances this might be mahogany or cedar. Practice varied from workshop to workshop and from period to period, and a guide can give only clues not answers.

BOOKS

The comprehensive book on all aspects of old English furniture is *The Dictionary of English Furniture*, by Percy Macquoid and Ralph Edwards. It is in three large volumes, copiously illustrated, and was first issued in 1927. A further edition, revised and enlarged by Ralph Edwards, was published in 1954.

An excellent guide to the period 1720–1820 is *Georgian Furniture*, issued by the Victoria and Albert Museum, 1951.*

A standard work on French furniture is *Les Ébénistes du XVIIIe Siècle*, by Comte François de Salverte, of which the fourth edition was published in Paris and Brussels in 1953. Also written in French, but less exhaustive and cheaper in price is *Les Meubles Français du XVIIIe Siècle*, by Pierre Verlet. It is in two volumes: i, *Menuiserie*, ii, *Ébénisterie*, published in Paris in 1956.* In English the Wallace Collection, London, *Catalogue of French Furniture*, by F. J. B. Watson, issued in 1956, contains a great deal of information and many illustrations.*

Part II

POTTERY AND PORCELAIN

CHAPTER SIX

Pottery

POTTERY is defined as earthenware and includes *Faience*, or *Majolica*, creamware and, according to many authorities, a near-porcelain variety called stoneware. It is the commoner type of chinaware; the features that place it apart from porcelain are that it is opaque, and that the glaze does not combine with the paste, or clay body.

The origins of the making of pottery are lost in antiquity, and date from when Primitive Man found that the heat of a fire would harden clay. So far as the modern collector is concerned little is available that was made before the sixteenth century, although a considerable number of earlier examples can be studied in museums. They are seen to be of simple shapes, mostly in the form of jugs; sometimes with decorative patterns cut or impressed into the red or buff clay; with patterns rubbed on or dribbled in wet clay (slip) of a contrasting colour or with designs stamped on pads of clay stuck on the article. Many are coloured with transparent glazes made from lead, in shades of yellow, brown or green. The shapes used varied from place to place and from century to century, and it is not always possible to name where or when a piece was made. Kilns with fragments of broken ware have been excavated, and these are a guide.

CHAPTER SEVEN

English pottery

THE type of pottery described in the previous chapter continued to be made in all parts of England throughout the seventeenth, eighteenth and nineteenth centuries, and much is still being made by the so-called *studio potters*. Among the more important later centres that have been identified with certainty, are: London (known as *Metropolitan Ware*); Wrotham, Kent; and Staffordshire, where the names of Toft, Simpson and Malkin are the best known. A further technique, known as *sgraffito* and consisting of decoration incised through a coating of light-coloured slip to a dark body, was practised in north Devonshire and other places.

John Astbury and Thomas Whieldon of Staffordshire were the foremost potters in the middle of the eighteenth century, and their output comprised wares of all the types that were then known. In particular, Whieldon's name is linked with wares with pale-coloured transparent glazes including early versions of the famous Toby Jug, and similar types were made by Ralph Wood and his son, also named Ralph. Astbury is noted for pieces made from red clay, either engine-turned on a lathe or with white clay ornaments in relief. These two men led the way to the perfecting of lead-glazed pottery, a step which was the achievement of Josiah Wedgwood. Wedgwood was a good practical potter, he had been for a few years in partnership with Whieldon, but was a better business man, and his cream-coloured lead-glazed earthenware, known from 1765 as *Queen's Ware*, was so successful that it competed with porcelain, and was imitated not only by other English makers but also all over the Continent of Europe. The closest imitator in England was the factory at Leeds, Yorkshire, which approached the high quality of Wedgwood's products, but often used original patterns. Much of Wedgwood's creamware was decorated by his own men in Staffordshire, or at a workshop he had for a time in London at Chelsea, but a quantity was sent to Liverpool to be ornamented by a newly invented process. This was by means of engravings printed on paper and transferred to the china article; quick, cheap and effective, it was typical of Wedgwood to test the possibilities of something as novel and promising. For the collector it is reassuring to know that the majority of Wedgwood ware is marked.

Early in the nineteenth century came the introductions of pieces decorated with *lustre*, both silver- and copper-coloured, and there was a great variety among the finished products. Silver lustre on a canary-yellow ground is the rarest, but silver in conjunction with underglaze blue, especially if the latter is a sporting subject, is sought after and expensive. Whole tea-sets were made at one period, each piece covered completely with a thin film of silver lustre, and they were a passable imitation of the real thing for those who could not afford to buy the genuine metal. Copper-lustred pieces have been made since about 1800 and production has been continuous for some 150 years; which explains why so many 'early nineteenth-century' specimens are obtainable.

Although creamware continued to be made, white-glazed pottery was developed from 1780 to compete with porcelain and was produced in great quantities by many makers. At first it had decoration printed solely in underglaze blue, but later developments included a wide range of colours. Whole services were made, and Spode, Wedgwood and Davenport (all of Staffordshire) were among the more prominent of the hundreds of names associated with it. The earlier blue-printed ware is very well finished and some of the patterns are most attractive; a few, including the willow-pattern, are still being made.

One of the most popular introductions of the first half of the nineteenth century was *ironstone china*, said to contain ironstone slag in its composition and certainly very strong. The heavy ware, almost unbreakable, was both cheap and showy. It was made in the form of domestic pieces with pseudo-oriental decoration in vivid blues and reds, and many of the big dinner-services are still being used. Sets of jugs, with handles in the shape of dragons, were made also and are not uncommon.

A style of decoration that is occasionally seen, particularly on jugs and tankards, is known as *mocha*, from a resemblance to a type of quartz of that name, and has brown moss-like blotches on it. The stains were made with the aid of tobacco-juice and hops, and doubtless gave pleasure to the potters making it.

Children were catered for from about 1830 with small plates printed with moral rhymes and other suitable subjects. Many were made in Staffordshire, but some came from Stockton-on-Tees, Co. Durham.

Enoch Wood and John Walton were prominent among makers of figures, many of them of small size and coloured in opaque enamels with green predominating. Many of Walton's bear an impressed stamp with the name of the maker. Later pieces, introduced in about 1850, are the well-known Staffordshire chimneypiece ornaments in the form of portrait-figures, often unrecognizable without the name painted on the front of the base, ranging from politicians to murderers.

Much of the nineteenth-century ware was marked by the makers, but often only with initials which do not help the collector very much. Printed pieces usually have the name of the pattern.

Stoneware. Stoneware is a very hard non-porous type of pottery, introduced into England in the sixteenth century from Germany. A feature of the ware is that it was glazed by putting common salt into the kiln while it was being fired; thus arises the term *salt-glazed stoneware*. The resulting pottery is hard, strong and water-tight, and it can be made into objects much thinner in body than can ordinary clay pottery.

Nottingham was a big centre for making stoneware from the late seventeenth century, and pieces with a hard grey body and a brown glaze of orange-peel texture came from there. Many such pieces bear names and dates. Other factories nearby in Derbyshire made similar wares.

A factory at Fulham, a suburb of London, was founded by

John Dwight in 1671. A number of pieces made by him, after two centuries in the possession of his family and now in the British and Victoria and Albert Museums, are extraordinarily well modelled, and it has been suggested that they are the work of the wood-carver and sculptor, Grinling Gibbons. Dwight claimed to have invented a method of making porcelain, but nothing resembling our modern meaning of the term can be attributed to him.

In Staffordshire, a red stoneware in imitation of some imported from China, was made by two Dutch brothers named Elers, who had worked at one time with Dwight at Fulham. By 1725 Dwight's greyish stoneware had been improved in colour until it was nearly white, and it was not long before this excellent salt-glazed material was being potted in quantity in the Staffordshire towns, in Liverpool, and elsewhere. Most of the ware, which was made not only into domestic articles but also figures, was ornamented with raised patterns, and the thin smear of glaze with which it was covered did not clog the delicate lines as a flowing lead-glaze would have done. Both overglaze and underglaze colours were used with great effect.

While white stoneware was finally unable to withstand the competition of Queen's Ware and porcelain, a further refinement of materials and technique enabled Wedgwood to produce with it his celebrated *jasper ware*. This is the pottery from which were made the thousands of relief portraits, plaques and vases that spread the name of their inventor and maker throughout the world. In addition to this ware, most familiar when coloured blue but made also in pale shades of yellow, lilac and green Wedgwood developed a black stoneware (*basaltes*), a red stoneware (*rosso antico*) and a buff-coloured (*cane ware*), all of which contributed to the fame and expansion of Staffordshire.

It is as well to remember that the descendants of Josiah Wedgwood are still making jasper and basaltes wares, and have done so continuously since the eighteenth century. The oldest examples reveal their age by the superior fineness of their modelling and the velvet-like smoothness of their surface.

Brown stoneware was made throughout the nineteenth century, but the productions are far from exciting. Flasks in the form of politicians and pistols were made, and a large number of jugs in imitation of seventeenth-century originals often deceive collectors.

Tin-glazed Earthenware. Sometime before 1600, with help from Continental potters and in imitation of Continental wares, English potters were able to make a great advance. It was by using an opaque white glaze on which coloured designs could be painted; a method originating in Italy. This type of pottery, glazed with a composition based on oxide of tin, which was available readily in England, is known as delftware from the similar ware made at Delft in Holland; although the latter town did not become connected with pottery-making until some time after English manufacture had started. The beginner has to beware of confusing English delftware with Dutch Delftware; a confusion that is not restricted to the verbal sense. For, it was emigrant Dutch potters who came to England and started making tin-glazed earthenware in the second half of the sixteenth century.

The first Dutch potters settled at Norwich, but nothing of their work has been identified positively. The earliest ware of the type is a series of brightly coloured jugs, named after the village in Kent where one was once kept in the church, West Malling, near Maidstone. One of these 'Malling' jugs has a silver mount dated 1550, and others bear later dates between then and 1600.

Queen Elizabeth I was petitioned by two Dutch potters, named Jaspar Andries and Jacob Janson, to allow them to settle and work in England, and it is believed that Janson set up a pottery in London in 1571. An early English dated piece of pottery now in the London Museum is a dish painted in colours with what appears to be the Tower of London, the date 1600, and an inscription reading 'The Rose is Red The Leaves are Grene God Save Elizabeth Our Queene'. It seems probable that this is of London manufacture but the colours used and style of painting are very like those on ware made on the Continent at the time.

A further surviving group of wares is dated about 1630, and consists of a number of mugs bearing English names and of shapes unlike current foreign types. Whereas these and earlier wares show, if anything, an Italian influence in the style and colouring of their decoration, the productions that followed were copied as closely as possible from Chinese porcelain; which by 1640–50 was coming to England in sufficient quantity to be a serious rival. Not only was Oriental porcelain being brought to England, but the other countries of Europe also imported it and their potteries in turn set out to imitate the newcomer.

It is clear that with pottery being made in England by Dutch potters copying Chinese originals and the same subjects being copied by the Dutch in their own country, it cannot be an easy matter to distinguish between the two wares. No English wares are marked, and it is agreed that only those of the seventeenth century of certain types and bearing English names or inscriptions can be accepted reasonably as originating in London. Among such pieces are a number of wine-bottles with dates from 1637 to 1672, and painted also with the names of wines: 'Claret', 'Sack' and 'Whit' (White). On these the painting is very sparse and the white body is often tinged with pale pink; a feature of tin-glaze. Allied to these bottles are a number of dishes, candlesticks, vases and other pieces, completely unpainted but of which many show the same slightly pink glaze. Also with this characteristic are pieces painted with the coats-of-arms of London companies, in particular the Company of Apothecaries with their motto 'Opiferque Per Orbem Dicor' found on shaped flat pill-slabs.

During the seventeenth century were produced a great number of large dishes, called sometimes 'blue-dash' chargers from their borders being painted with a series of dashes in blue. They are skilfully painted in colours, and the subjects on them vary from Adam and Eve to scenes of the reigning monarch and his family. Many are dated, but there is ground for viewing some of the dates with suspicion; one dish showing Charles I and his family is dated 1653 although he had died eight years earlier, and another of '1614' is of a type considered to have been made not less than thirty years after. No reason has yet been found to account for these discrepancies.

Until about 1660 London delftware was made at Aldgate or Southwark, but shortly afterwards potteries were opened in Lambeth, which soon expanded and became the most important in England. By this time some of the Southwark potters had started a works at Brislington, near Bristol, and within a further period there were potteries operating in Bristol itself and in Wincanton, Somerset, and by 1710 in Liverpool. A group of Lambeth potters was working in Glasgow in 1748, and potteries were operating in Ireland at Dublin (from about 1737) and Limerick (from 1762).

These various potteries not only owed their beginnings to the efforts and skill of men from their fellow-manufactories, but these very men did much the same work in their new homes as they had done in their old. The variations in clays, glazes and colours between one factory and another are slight, and the wares must often be apportioned to each factory on other evidence. Excavations made on the site of former potteries, and pieces that have remained in the hands of descendants of known potters and painters, and similarly documented specimens give a more reliable picture. Unfortunately, there is still not enough accumulated evidence to make certain identification possible in the majority of instances.

All the English delftware potteries in the eighteenth century copied principally Chinese imported ware, with a marked predominance of painting in blue. A quantity of commemorative pieces was made, and includes many recording coronations. Other inscribed pieces bear initials and dates, but rarely, if ever, was anything resembling a factory mark employed. Tin-glazed earthenware was enormously popular in its day as can be seen from the great number of surviving specimens, but towards the end of the eighteenth century it succumbed to the superior merit and lower cost of creamware.

CHAPTER EIGHT

Continental pottery

WITH the aid of methods learned from Near Eastern potters the Moorish conquerors of Spain established a number of potteries. There, they produced an earthenware decorated brilliantly in a copper-coloured lustre, known as *Hispano-Moresque* ware. With the reconquest of Spain and the expelling of the Moors, the making of this and other pottery was continued by the Spaniards themselves. These wares reached Italy in the fifteenth century by way of Majorca, and the name of that island, where they were supposed wrongly to have been made, was given to them in a corrupted form: *majolica*.

Italian-made majolica, a tin-glazed earthenware that is comparable to the faience of France, the Delft of Holland and the delftware of England, was at first an imitation of the imported product, but it soon achieved a style of its own. It was made principally between the fifteenth and seventeenth centuries, and although some was made after the latter date it has neither the interest nor the importance of the earlier pieces. The Italian ware was sent to other European countries, and inspired their potters in turn to produce ware of a comparable high standard. The painting of majolica is its greatest beauty and the artists who did it were masters of both line and colour. Not only were the nearly flat surfaces of dishes used for coloured pictures that remind us of the glory of the Italy of the early sixteenth century, but the round pot, known as an *albarello*, was equally lavishly and diversely painted. The chemist's shop of the time was a general meeting-place as well as a medical emporium, and the shelves held numbers of colourful *albarelli* containing drugs and ointments.

Among the places famous for their majolica potteries are: Faenza, Florence, Caffagiolo, Urbino, Castel Durante, Gubbio, Savona, Siena, Deruta and Venice, all of which are in the northern half of Italy, but there were many less-important centres in both north and south. The subject of majolica is a very wide one; much study has been given to it and many books written about it during the past hundred years. Only rarely are fine specimens to be obtained and, understandably, when they are, they command high prices.

Italian majolica was exported to all the countries of Europe, and greatly affected the wares they made. In some instances, Italian potters were induced to settle abroad and teach local men how to improve their work. This occurred at Antwerp, in particular, and with the invasion of Flanders by the Spaniards in the late sixteenth century the potters fled northwards to Holland.

Dutch tin-glazed pottery, known by the name of the town of Delft where it became established eventually, was made in great quantities and much was sent to England. Not only was there a big trade in dishes and other domestic wares, but Dutch tiles were sent also. These were of sufficient importance to become a separate branch of pottery-making; some men made them to the exclusion of all else, and sets of tiles were painted to be placed together and form pictures.

Germany, also, had numerous potteries making tin-glazed wares, and those of Hamburg, Frankfurt, Hanau and Bayreuth were outstanding centres; the first-named, together with Nuremburg, being noted for making the great glazed and decorated pottery stoves used for heating rooms in many Continental countries. Much of the output resembled the earthenware being made elsewhere at the time, and much remains confused with contemporary English and Dutch work. Many German and Swiss potters made lead-glazed wares with slip and *sgraffito* decoration; much of it inscribed and dated. There were big centres for the making of stoneware at Cologne and Siegburg, the latter near Bonn. Much of the output was decorated elaborately with impressed patterns, and a large quantity of *bellarmines* was made; these are jugs with fat bodies and short thin necks, the head of a bearded man impressed on the front.

Bernard Palissy, whose life-span embraced almost the whole

of the sixteenth century, made dishes and other pieces modelled with lizards, shells, leaves and fishes. The clay of which these are made is whitish, and Palissy and his followers covered it effectively with coloured transparent glazes. It is said that 'no class of pottery has been so widely copied for fraud'.

The white lead-glazed earthenware of St Porchaire was decorated in an unusual manner by impressing it in patterns with small metal stamps and filling the marks with coloured clays. This small sixteenth-century pottery has had a chequered literary history, and a century ago was the subject of speculation and bitter argument among experts; first stated to have been at Lyons, then at Beauvais, and again Oiron, it has been decided that it was actually located at St Porchaire, north of Bordeaux. Only just over sixty pieces of the ware survive, and most of them are in museums. It has been faked, and the English Minton factory made exact copies of known examples.

Other French potters were affected closely by Italian work, but by the seventeenth century the factory at Rouen was making a tin-glazed majolica of character with decoration in red and blue. Potteries at Marseilles, Moustiers, Strasbourg, and elsewhere shortly became prominent, and today French faience is recognized as having a distinction of its own that rivals porcelain. It was well made and well painted, the shapes were interesting and often strikingly unusual.

The Swedish potteries at Marieberg and Rörstrand made excellent wares in original shapes with fine decoration towards the end of the eighteenth century. At about the same date a Norwegian factory at Herrebøe made some equally interesting pieces. Productions from these factories are rare outside Scandinavia.

All types of wares were made in Portugal, but most are indistinguishable from those of Spain, Italy and Holland. A century ago, a pottery was founded at Caldas da Rainha by Manuel Mafra, and has made imitations of Palissy-ware and other colour-glazed pieces ever since. Some bear the maker's mark, others do not.

1. *Above:* English seventeenth-century oak and walnut furniture:
tall-back walnut chairs, 1675; chairs with upholstered backs
and seats and turned legs, 1650; oak table with carved freize,
1650; oak cupboard, 1630; oak panelling, 1620.

2. *Below:* English eighteenth-century mahogany furniture:
dining chairs, 1750; dining table, 1790; sideboard, 1790.

3. *Above:* English early eighteenth-century furniture: bureau decorated in red and gold lacquer, 1705; walnut chair with cabriole legs and turned stretchers, 1710; carved walnut chair with needlework cover to back and seat, 1725; mahogany and walnut table with carved freize and cabriole legs, 1750.

4. *Below:* Late eighteenth/early nineteenth-century English furniture: sabre-legged mahogany chair, 1810; child's chair of painted beechwood, 1835; inlaid mahogany sideboard, 1795; rosewood chair, 1825.

5. *Above:* Chinese porcelain: figure of Kwan Yin (Goddess of Mercy) decorated with splashes of green, yellow and aubergine (brown-purple), K'ang Hsi; plate painted in blue with the coat-of-arms of James, first Earl of Charlemont, who was created an Earl in 1763; Tê-Hua white porcelain figure of Kwan Yin, eighteenth century; small bowl with famille rose decoration, late eighteenth century; wine bottle with famille verte decoration, K'ang Hsi, late seventeenth century.

6. *Below:* Japanese works of art: dagger with bronze handle (*Kodzuka*) inlaid with a pattern of fishes by Ichijoshi Hirotoshi; two-fold screen in Shibayama work on gold lacquer in a carved ivory frame; circular sword mount (Tsuba) of iron inset with gold; ivory carving of two mice with a hen's egg; gold lacquer box and cover in the form of Daikoku (a mythological character), by Yoshikawa Joshinsai; wood carving of a cat seated on a melon and being dragged along by seven rats, signed by Homin; a gold lacquer Inro with a design of flying cranes, by Kajikawa, with a lacquer Ojime and a flat circular Netsuke.

7. *Above:* Continental eighteenth-century porcelain: Furstenburg bust of the poet Horace, 1810; Dresden dish painted with flowers, 1760; Zurich tea caddy, 1770; Dresden group of two lovers, 1750; Dresden saucer painted with a mock-Oriental scene, 1735; Sèvres plate, 1760; Doccia needlecase, 1760.

8. *Below:* Late seventeenth-century Mortlake tapestry of boys playing at acrobatics.

CHAPTER NINE

Persia and neighbouring countries

IN Persia and other Near East countries pottery had been made for many centuries, and while the majority of Europe was in a state of barbarism, attractive wares were being made with brilliantly coloured glazes and with designs incised or painted. The Persians rediscovered the art of tin-glazing, a technique used by the Assyrians, and were masters in the use of coloured lustres by the end of the twelfth century. Both of these processes reached Europe later by way of the Moors in Spain.

Many types of Chinese wares were exported to the Near East countries, and there was a constant interchange of ideas; the Chinese learned of painting in underglaze blue from the Persian potters at Kashan, and the Persians made imitations of their favourite Chinese celadon glazes. Following the important Persian Exhibition held in London in 1931, scholars have turned their attention to the earlier wares, and attempts are being made to trace a sequence of styles and to discover exactly where the various types were made.

Excavations carried out at the end of the nineteenth century first revealed the beauty of these Islamic wares which had then been long forgotten. Ironically, beautiful as so many of them are, most have been restored from fragments found discarded in rubbish-pits in Persia and Egypt. Good examples are, understandably, rare, and poor ones skilfully made up from two or more articles with a generous helping of plaster and paint are to be guarded against.

Most of the wares made in Persian and nearby pottery centres from the fourteenth century onwards are versions of earlier types and show less originality. Imitations of Ming blue-and-white, with thick glaze and a very runny blue, are sometimes mistaken for Chinese.

To the north-west of Persia, in Turkey, a distinctive pottery was made. It has a sandy body coated with white slip, decorated with painting of formal floral or leaf patterns outlined in black and coloured in a distinctive thick red, bright green and blue. It dates from about the sixteenth century. This ware was once thought to be of Persian origin, later said to have come from the Island of Rhodes and known as 'Rhodian' ware, but is now accepted as having been made principally at Isnik, a town to the south of Istanbul.

CHAPTER TEN

America

SOME of the earliest inhabitants of both North and South America were skilled and artistic potters, and examples of their work are to be found in museums; occasionally, they can be bought. In more modern times, in the days of John Smith and Pocahontas, there were still potters at work in America, and it would not have taken the European settlers long to find a suitable clay from which to make domestic pieces. In 1641 there is a record of James Pride, a potter at Salem, Massachusetts, and it is believed that others were operating in Jamestown, Virginia. Of these first craftsmen, and many that followed in their wake, there is a little to show except a written record of some of their names. They made useful everyday wares that served their purpose, were broken and discarded, and there was no particular reason to treasure them.

The picture changed little in the first three-quarters of the eighteenth century. The Crolius and Remney families were established at Potters' Hill, New York City; while at Burlington, New Jersey, Daniel Coxe made what he described as 'White Chiney Ware'. Newspapers of the period show that pottery and porcelain were imported in quantity from England and from the Far East, and the local potters were left to make little other than 'butter, water, pickle, oyster and chamber pots; milk pans of several sizes; jugs . . . mugs . . . bowls, porringers . . . cups', etc.

Very little has survived that can be dated positively as having been made before 1800, and in America. A bowl in the Brooklyn museum, of Pennsylvania red earthenware incised with the date 1775 is outstanding; in the same museum is a white pottery sauceboat, copied probably from a Liverpool imported example, decorated with Chinese landscapes in blue, made in Philadelphia. Examples of red clay domestic ware include baking dishes which are indistinguishable from their English originals; likewise, Pennsylvania dishes with *sgraffito* decoration closely similar to German country-made ones.

Salt-glazed stoneware was made for suitable articles, and a tall round butter churn by Clarkson Crolius Senior, made about 1800, belongs to the New York Historical Society. At about the same date a pottery was set up to make creamware to compete with imported Wedgwood, gave it the name of Tivoli Ware and advertised for orders and apprentices.

Authentic pieces of the early wares are extremely scarce; as it was purely utilitarian in purpose it was seldom, if ever, marked. The demand for anything sophisticated was met from abroad, until in the early nineteenth century, when conditions grew more settled in the land, and manufactories were started to supply the home market on a large scale.

Porcelain was made in about 1740 by a man named Andrew Duché, born in Philadelphia in 1710. A small bowl with Oriental-style underglaze blue decoration was discovered in 1946 and is assumed to be one of his experimental pieces. It is in a private collection in the United States. Thirty years later, two partners named Gouse Bonnin and George Anthony Morris started a factory in Philadelphia, but it is doubtful whether they made much true porcelain. The first successful commercial making of the ware was again in Philadelphia and owed its inception to a Quaker, William Ellis Tucker, who began to experiment in 1826. Tucker's porcelain was of good quality and included tea sets, vases and other pieces, many of which won awards at exhibitions in New York and elsewhere. The factory closed in 1838.

CHAPTER ELEVEN

Porcelain

PORCELAIN is subdivided into two kinds. The Oriental, true, or *hard-paste* porcelain was made first in the Far East and is composed of two natural ingredients—china-clay and china-stone—which form porcelain when they have been mixed together and heated to a temperature of 1,300 to 1,400 degrees Centigrade. The material formed in this way is extremely hard, white and translucent, and if chipped or broken shows a shiny and moist-looking fracture. So-called *soft-paste* or artificial porcelain is made from glass fused with clay or some other substance to make it opaque and produces a superficial imitation of true hard-paste; although difficult to manipulate, it does not need to be fired at such a high temperature. It differs in appearance from hard-paste in allowing colours to sink more into the glaze, and if broken or chipped shows a sugary granular fracture. A further type of soft-paste, *bone china*, was introduced in England in about 1800, and employs china-clay and china-stone combined with a white powder obtained from calcined bones. It is not as costly to make as hard-paste, is more manageable in manufacture and durable in use than soft-paste, and has remained to this day the most popular and esteemed English china.

All types of clay wares are put into their finished shape before being fired in a kiln, and there are three principal methods of doing this.

Moulding or Pressing: by pressing a thin cake of clay into a mould; for instance, for making plates.

Casting: by pouring liquefied clay into a plaster mould, leaving it for a stated time and then pouring away the surplus. In due course the article is removed from the mould. The plaster absorbs moisture where it is in contact with the wet clay, as it dries shrinkage takes place and they separate easily. Figures are built up from many separately moulded pieces which are then assembled by sticking them together with wet clay. The man who does this is called a *repairer*, and he scrapes away all signs of his work before the piece is fired. On some occasions these repairers used marks; at Bow, Plymouth and Worcester a Frenchman named Thibault rendered his name phonetically as T° which is sometimes found impressed or in raised letters.

Throwing: this is a very old way of working, and employs a flat circular table which revolves by foot-treadle or other means. It is used for the making of vases and bowls; manipulation by the hands of the craftsman aided by centrifugal force forms the article.

One further method used in primitive times, and occasionally today by studio potters, should be added: in this, vessels are built up with long ropes of clay coiled round and round. The coils are flattened on the surface, and it is claimed that this has the merit of producing wares without mechanical intervention that express more closely the mind and intention of the potter.

With hard-paste porcelain the ware can next be painted, glazed and then fired, but only a few colours (notably blue) will stand the great heat of the furnace. Most are applied after the glaze has been fired, and the piece is then re-fired at a lower temperature. Soft-paste porcelain is fired, glazed and re-fired, before it is painted and fired yet again. Underglaze colours can be used on soft-paste ware that has received its first firing, and is then in the state known as *biscuit*. At some factories particularly well-finished pieces were sold uncoloured and unglazed as biscuit-ware.

The marks of many factories were copied widely, and they are not a reliable guide for identification. The collector should aim at recognition by other signs, such as modelling and colouring and the type of paste, and treat marks as of secondary importance.

CHAPTER TWELVE

English porcelain factories

ENGLISH porcelain is, with the exception of Plymouth, all of soft-paste, and it is important for the collector to learn to recognize this feature. Like so many difficult things, it cannot be done at once; some are able to recognize it quickly and almost by intuition, but for most it is a matter of patience and experience.

Of the factories operating before 1785, Chelsea and Worcester were the most consistent in their use of marks but quite a large proportion of their output, like that of the other makers, is unmarked. Some of the factories copied the crossed swords of Dresden, and some copied each other. After 1785, the position grew better, but there were still more unmarked pieces than marked.

One feature of decorating should be mentioned: the practice of factories selling their ware, white and glazed, to men with decorating establishments of their own. This was not at all uncommon in the early days of porcelain-making, and the name of James Giles is among the best known of those doing this type of work. William Duesbury, later owner of the Derby factory and purchaser of both Chelsea and Bow, began his career similarly. There was a further outburst of activity of this nature early in the nineteenth century, when Nantgarw porcelain was painted in London by Randall and Robins. Men who worked in this way are known as 'outside decorators', because their workshops were unconnected with a particular factory.

Chelsea

A few cream jugs with the word 'Chelsea', a triangle and the date 1745 incised in the clay under the base before it was fired have been preserved. They prove that the works was in being by that year, and it has been argued that because the jugs are so well finished whoever made them had practised his skill for some time prior. A number of other pieces also marked with a scratched triangle are known, and to about the same early date belongs a mark in underglaze blue in the form of a trident intersecting a crown. Most of these wares were unpainted but glazed, and some show that French porcelain of the period was probably their inspiration as regards both the modelling and the glassy body.

1. Incised in the paste before it hardened, but has been faked.
1745–50

2. An anchor raised on an oval mound, sometimes with the anchor painted red.
1749–52

3. Painted in red; sometimes on the base of a piece, but often among the surface decoration of figures.
1752–58

An anchor in gold was used from 1758–69.

From 1749, the factory was managed by Nicholas Sprimont, originally a silversmith from Liége, and under his direction it reached great heights. The most important period lasted from 1752 until 1758, and includes three sales by auction of which the catalogues of two have survived. By means of these, many of the articles then made have been identified, and a clear idea gained of the diversity of pieces current. The most significant are the figures, many after Dresden but many original, and having ample individuality in modelling and colouring. By this time, most of the wares were painted at the factory, and the work of several artists with recognizably personal styles has been recorded. From the mark that was used this is known as the Red Anchor period, and W. B. Honey suggested that Chelsea was then responsible for 'perhaps the most beautiful porcelain material ever made'.

The following Gold Anchor period saw a trend to more ambitious pieces; large figures and groups, vases and costly table services, decorated in brilliant colourings and often heavily gilt. The factory eventually ceased to pay and was sold in 1769.

Bought by William Duesbury of Derby, it continued manufacturing until 1784, but the wares were not to be compared
with those of former days.

One speciality of Chelsea deserves a mention: the so-called
'Toys', or miniature pieces in the form of seals, scent-bottles,
snuff-boxes, etc., which were made in large numbers and remain
as popular today as they were in the 1760's. Of these, a few
miniature figures bear the anchor in red but none of the other
trifles has any mark. A scent-bottle, in the British Museum, is
dated 1759.

Bow

In 1744 a patent was taken out by Thomas Frye and a partner
for a method of making porcelain using a clay imported from
America. Four years later, Frye alone took out another patent
in which bone-ash was included as a further ingredient. It is
known that a man named George Arnold financed the company
until his death in 1751, but little is certain yet about the type of
ware produced before that date. Visual identification can be
confirmed with reasonable certainty; Bow was the first factory
to incorporate bone-ash in the paste used, and its presence can
be proved by simple chemical analysis. In 1753 the firm opened
a warehouse in Cornhill, in the City of London, and employed an
ex-navy man, John Bowcock, as clerk; some of Bowcock's account
books and papers have been preserved, although others have
since been lost, and they add a little to the meagre history known
at present.

Bow made many figures, but only rarely do they approach the
standards of modelling and painting of Chelsea. Contemporary
accounts reveal that they concentrated on tableware, and much
of this, decorated in underglaze blue, has survived. Many of the
earlier pieces were sold uncoloured, and those that were painted
often show decoration in the current Chinese and Japanese
styles. Many of the figures are after Dresden models, but a
number are original; mugs were a popular production and on
many of them the handle terminates in the shape of a heart where

it is joined to the body. The factory closed in 1776 after one of the later owners had died and the other had gone bankrupt, and like Chelsea it was bought by Duesbury of Derby. Many of the figures can be recognized by the use of a vivid purple-red colour used often to outline the scrolling on bases, and by an opaque blue enamel used for clothing, etc. The edges of plates and other pieces sometimes show small areas of brown staining where the glaze is thin or absent. There was no definite mark used on the factory's wares, but a number of different ones were used by painters. Most of the pieces are unmarked.

Derby

It has been suggested that the Derby factory was making porcelain as early as 1745, but the earliest actual evidence is a number of white cream jugs inscribed with the name of the town and the date 1750. William Duesbury, who had been a painter of figures bought in the white, became proprietor at some date before 1760, and Derby ware began to be advertised as 'the second Dresden'. Duesbury bought up the Longton Hall factory and also those at Bow and Chelsea; all three of which he closed eventually and concentrated his energies on Derby. On his death in 1786 he was succeeded by his son, and after some further changes the factory was bought by Robert Bloor and closed finally in 1848.

The earliest pieces are unmarked and not easy to recognize; the figures have unglazed bases with the glaze shrinking away from the edge, and a funnel-shaped hole in the centre. Later wares include a large number of figures, usually made in pairs, of which the characteristic feature is the presence under the base of three or four dirty patches, each about half an inch in diameter, where the piece stood on flat pads of clay in the kiln. Although these patch-marks appear occasionally on the products of other factories, their presence is consistent with Derby and they are rarely missing. A further feature that distinguishes most of these figures is the use of an opaque turquoise green paint in the decoration; a green that is often stained brown.

Shortly after 1770 groups and figures were made and sold unglazed, as *biscuit*. These were very highly finished, for there would be no glaze or colour to hide defects, and were sold at higher prices than their painted counterparts. Most of the figures made at this time were marked with a number under the base, which corresponds with published lists giving the title and selling-price.

The following period, from 1784 to 1811, is known as Crown-Derby, when the wares bore a mark incorporating a crown. Fine tablewares were then a speciality, and many had elaborate coloured and gilt borders surrounding a carefully painted landscape scene. A number of painters were employed, each specializing in his own subject.

Between 1811 and the closing of the factory much tableware was painted vividly in pseudo-Japanese patterns, but some of the earlier styles were continued.

4. In red or gold. 'Chelsea-Derby' 1770–84

5. Incised under the base of figures; a list of the mould numbers is in Haslem's book *The Old Derby China Factory* (1876). 1770–1800

6. Incised or in colour. 1770–1848

Lund's Bristol

In 1748 a porcelain factory was started at Bristol, where it was found possible to make an excellent soft-paste ware with the aid of a stone, steatite or soapstone found in Cornwall, as one of the ingredients. The incorporation of soapstone in the paste produced a china that could be potted thinly, that would withstand con-

tact with boiling water, and was therefore particularly suitable
for making domestic pieces such as cups, cream jugs, and teapots.
The Bristol factory was started by Benjamin Lund, a brass-
founder, and its wares are referred to as *Lund's Bristol* to distinguish them from those of the later Bristol hard-paste porcelain
works. Lund's china can seldom be distinguished from that of
early Worcester, but a few figures of Chinamen and some sauce-
boats have been found with the word 'BRISTOLL' moulded on them
in raised lettering. Some delicately made small pieces painted
very neatly in Chinese patterns in colours or underglaze blue
are assigned to Lund's period, but as the factory was in being
for only a short period it is not surprising that pieces are now
rare.

Worcester

Early in 1752 the right to use Lund's soapstone formula was
purchased by a newly constituted company in Worcester, and
the well-known factory came into being. One of the principal
shareholders in the Worcester company was a local physician of
eminence, Dr John Wall, and his name has been given to the
period 1752 to 1783, during which the factory produced its most
famous output.

At first, domestic ware with underglaze blue decoration was
the principal output, but by 1760 the making of more ambitious
pieces of high quality, both as regards shape and colouring, was
being carried on. Shortly before, the process of decorating by
the use of printed designs transferred to the article, *transfer-
printing*, had been introduced. The finely engraved designs, many
of them adapted by Robert Hancock from the work of French
and English artists of the time, were printed effectively in overglaze colours of black, lilac or red. Soon, it was found possible
to print in underglaze blue, and a large amount decorated in this
manner was made and sold in the next twenty years.

About 1769, when it is believed some of the redundant Chelsea
painters were given employment at Worcester, a style of painting
in panels on a coloured ground was initiated. The grounds used

are a plain dark blue, a dark blue in the form of overlapping scales known as *scale-blue*, red and yellow in the same manner, a rich apple green, a plain yellow and a plain sky blue. All these grounds were enriched further with gilt patterns as well as designs of figures in costume, exotic birds or bouquets of flowers; a display of them makes it clear why they have been famous for so long, and why they are expensive today.

For a short period about 1770, figures were made at Worcester, but although they are painted in typical Worcester colours they are stiff and unnatural in appearance and it is assumed that they were not a success at the time. They are very rare, and have been identified only recently after masquerading as the work of other factories for nearly two hundred years.

Worcester china, marked or unmarked, is remarkable for its slightly grey appearance and for the fact that the glaze shrinks away at the edges; particularly on the insides of the foot-rims of plates, cups, and similarly constructed pieces. This feature has never been imitated successfully, in spite of the fact that Worcester was much copied at the time it was made, and has continued to be faked ever since.

In 1783 the factory was bought by Thomas Flight and managed by his sons, a visit was paid to it shortly by King George III and Queen Charlotte, and a complete change in the style of ware began to take place. The new productions were of simple shapes, but very finely painted in the manner of miniatures. Popular subjects were groups of feathers or sea-shells carefully painted in natural colours. The china itself was highly glazed and often modelled with borders of 'pearls', left white or heavily gilt. On the death of one of Flight's sons in 1791 Martin Barr became a partner, and the firm became Flight and Barr; other changes involving the style of the firm took place in 1807 and 1813.

Robert Chamberlain left Flight's about 1783, and after a period in which he decorated porcelain bought from other factories, started his own works in Worcester. His sons were skilled painters, and they decorated in a manner similar to that of the older company. Chamberlain ware is of a marked grey tint and the paste is often lumpy, much showy gilding was used and a salmon-pink ground was very popular.

Thomas Grainger started a further Worcester factory in 1801, and produced wares similar to those of the other two factories. Finally, Chamberlain's formed a partnership with the original factory and this became eventually the Royal Worcester Porcelain Company, which is still in production.

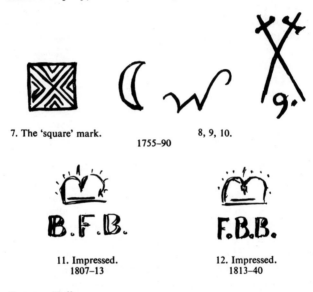

7. The 'square' mark.

8, 9, 10.
1755–90

11. Impressed.
1807–13

12. Impressed.
1813–40

Longton Hall

This Staffordshire china works was started in about 1750 and lasted for only ten years. Its productions and its very existence were almost forgotten until the year 1881, when newspaper advertisements relating to it were discovered and reprinted. Further details published in 1957, including some of the original documents and excavations on the actual factory site, confirmed the origin of many pieces that had been allocated to it.

The wares are made of a greyish paste, mostly glazed with

what has been described as a covering resembling 'candle-grease', and many of the larger productions were sold with fire-cracks, bubbles and other blemishes. In spite of this, it has both charm and interest. Many of the designs of both tableware and figures are original, and the painting is occasionally of a high standard.

An underglaze colour of a noticeably strong dark blue was used, and this was overpainted sometimes with a thick white enamel to give a lace-like effect. An underglaze dark purple was also employed occasionally.

Many Longton Hall pieces are still confused with those from other factories, notably Liverpool. Most of it is not marked.

Liverpool

The city of Liverpool was the seat of a number of porcelain factories during the eighteenth century although evidence of their activities and their productions is scanty. Richard Chaffers is known to have made a ware similar to that of Worcester and containing soapstone as an ingredient. Zachariah Barnes is said to have been the maker of pieces printed in underglaze blue of a dark shade. Identified Liverpool porcelain is occasionally of good quality, but most of it is commonplace domestic ware. No figures have been found.

John Sadler and Guy Green of Liverpool claimed that they had invented a process for decorating pottery and porcelain with transfer-prints. In 1756 they said they had done this four years before, but they did not trouble to patent their process and it is open to argument whether they were the first to use it. Local porcelain was decorated by them, as well as ware from factories farther distant, and a small number of surviving Liverpool pieces are printed in several colours.

Lowestoft

A small factory was started in this Suffolk town in 1757, and continued in operation until 1802. In the past it received attention out of all proportion to the merit of its productions, and

through a mistake in a book published in 1863 a very large amount
of Chinese hard-paste porcelain was accredited to it. In spite of
the fact that this has been proved a fallacy, much Chinese ware
of the once-disputed type is still called 'Lowestoft'; not only in
England, but also in America.

Lowestoft ware is similar to that of Bow, and the factory is
said to have been started by a man who smuggled himself into
the Bow works and learned the secrets of their manufacture.
This story may or may not be true, but the two porcelains are
very alike in appearance and both contain bone-ash. Much
domestic ware painted in underglaze blue was made at Lowestoft,
and is indistinguishable from that made at the London factory.
Many of the pieces were decorated in colours, and a few figures
are claimed to have been made.

One feature of the productions during forty-five years is the
large number of commemorative pieces that were made. They
range from small tablets honouring a birth or death, to sets of
tankards with the name of the alehouse for which they were
made. They are interesting, much sought after and rare, many
having gone to museums.

Plymouth

In 1768 William Cookworthy, a Plymouth chemist, took out
a patent for the making of true hard-paste porcelain using
ingredients he had found in Cornwall. He opened a factory at
Plymouth in that year, and two years later transferred it to Bristol
where Richard Champion became manager until he bought the
concern in 1773. The earlier porcelain made at Plymouth is often
smoke-stained and mis-shapen, and the underglaze blue sometimes used is more like a blue-black. After the move to Bristol
many of the same faults appear, but less frequently, and the
majority of the pieces stand comparison with other wares of the
period. Many of the shapes of tablewares are from Sèvres
models, but some of the figures are original in design and their
painting is usually very accomplished. A number of highly
decorative services were made at Bristol for presentation by

Champion to his friends, and another feature of the factory was some small biscuit plaques carefully modelled with flowers and other ornament in relief round a portrait bust, or a coat-of-arms. The thirty or so recorded plaques of this description include five with portraits of Benjamin Franklin, and one with George Washington.

In 1781, the patent was sold to a group of Staffordshire potters who opened a factory called New Hall at Longport, Staffordshire. The mark at Plymouth was the alchemists' sign for tin, like a figure four, in red; and at Bristol an 'X' in blue.

Caughley

A manufactory was built at Caughley (pronounced 'Coffley') near Bridgnorth in Shropshire, by Thomas Turner in 1772, and porcelain was made there soon after that date. It was called at the time, and still is, *Salopian* ware, and is very similar in appearance to Worcester, which it copied. Much of it was printed in underglaze blue and sometimes shows a yellow or brownish tone if held up to the light, whereas Worcester is more often inclined to appear a pale green. Turner is credited with producing the original version of the favoured 'willow-pattern', which was copied on both pottery and porcelain by innumerable other makers, and remains popular today.

The factory was bought by John Rose of Coalport in 1799, and eventually the two were merged and the Caughley works closed.

New Hall

In 1781 a group of Staffordshire potters bought the Plymouth hard-paste patent from Champion of Bristol, and opened a factory at Longport, Staffordshire, which they called New Hall. They made simple tablewares with cottage-type simple decoration and are said to have made more ambitious painted pieces as well. Many of the productions are marked under the base with 'N' or 'N°' in red and a pattern number. The factory closed in 1835.

Davenport

A factory at Longport in Staffordshire was operated by successive members of the Davenport family from 1793 until 1882, and during much of the time porcelain was made. The ware is not especially distinguished and varies in quality, but some good porcelain-painters worked there at times. Two of them, James Holland and Joshua Cristall became well-known water-colour artists. Much Davenport china is unmarked, but some pieces bear the name of the factory with or without an anchor, and sometimes with the word 'Longport' added. The mark was at first impressed, but later was printed.

Minton

Thomas Minton, an engraver of designs for printing on china, started a factory in 1793 and the firm continues today. He made good bone china, but it is on the productions of his descendants that the fame of the firm rests; they concentrated on making close copies of old Sèvres, which were bought by those who could not afford the extremely high prices realized by the latter in the mid-nineteenth century and later. In 1870, a Frenchman, Marc-Louis Solon, introduced a technique of decorating china by painting and modelling with white slip on a dark background, known as pâte-sur-pâte: 'clay on clay'. Solon is equally remembered for forming a large collection of English pottery and porcelain and for writing a number of early books on the subject.

Pinxton

A small factory was started at Pinxton, Derbyshire, by William Billingsley, who was later at Nantgarw. Billingsley was at Pinxton from 1796 to 1801, and made a particularly fine glassy soft-paste porcelain which was well decorated. After he left, the quality of the ware declined, and the factory closed in 1813.

Coalport

This Shropshire factory, known first as Coalbrookdale, was started by John Rose in 1796, and three years later merged with the nearby Caughley works. Some of its best-known productions are heavily encrusted with flowers in relief; inkstands, vases, dishes and even teapots were decorated in this manner. The Coalport factory made china of good quality throughout the nineteenth century, and some of its imitations of early Sèvres were good enough to deceive experts for many years. Copies of Chelsea, including the famous goat-and-bee jug, are slightly less dangerous but sometimes catch people off their guard.

After many vicissitudes the factory was removed to Staffordshire. Modern pieces bear a mark incorporating the date 1750, which leads many owners into thinking that they were made in that year.

Spode

Josiah Spode carried on a pottery started by his father of the same name, and in or about 1800 began to make porcelain. Josiah Spode II is credited with the introduction and popularization of bone china, which shortly became the standard ware for most English factories. Spode's porcelain was of excellent quality, but heavily decorated and gilt; much use was made of a dark underglaze blue, an effective background for elaborate tracery in gold.

The business eventually came into the ownership of the partner of Josiah Spode III, William Taylor Copeland, later became Copeland and Garrett, and is continued today as Copeland's by direct descendants. The firm is said to have been the first to introduce the off-white smooth biscuit ware known as *Parian*, from its resemblance to the marble of Paros, an island in the Aegean Sea, used by the ancient Greeks. The Parian china was used to make statuettes after the work of contemporary sculptors, and was extremely popular. Examples were shown at the Great Exhibition of 1851, and manufacture continued for many years after that date. Many pieces bear the word 'SPODE', painted, printed or impressed.

Wedgwood

The Wedgwood factory at Etruria made porcelain for a few

years from 1812. It was decorated in colours, and has the name
of the firm printed on the base in red, blue or gold.

Nantgarw and Swansea

A factory at Nantgarw, near Cardiff, the capital city of Wales,
was started in 1813 by William Billingsley, potter and china-
painter. A porcelain of remarkable whiteness and translucence was
made, but it was difficult to manipulate and failures in firing
made it costly to produce. Within a year it was transferred to
Swansea where attempts were made to improve the ware, making
it easier to fire while preserving its appearance. A return was made
shortly to Nangarw, but after a few years Billingsley went to
work at Coalport and probably only decorating was done at
Nantgarw. In 1822, Rose bought up the moulds and stock,
and took them to his Coalport factory.

The principal output was in the form of tablewares, but vases
were made also. Much of the ware was sold undecorated, and
then painted in London. It is sought eagerly today, and is very
expensive. The mark is the name of the factory impressed, with
the letters 'c.w.' below.

Rockingham

A factory at Swinton, Yorkshire, on the estate of the Marquis
of Rockingham, is known by the name of that nobleman who
became its patron. Porcelain was made there from about 1820
and lavishly decorated vases and tablewares bear the factory
mark: a griffin from the Rockingham crest. Extravagant decoration on good-quality porcelain gained the firm royal patronage
and the title 'Manufacturer to the King' in 1830. Plain and
attractively-modelled biscuit figures and groups were made, as
well as pastille-burners in the form of cottages and castles, and
small figures of poodles. The factory closed in 1842.

CHAPTER THIRTEEN

Continental porcelain

CONTINENTAL porcelain differs essentially from English in that it was in nearly every instance, either at first or eventually, hard-paste. Even those factories that began with pseudo-glass soft-paste turned in the end to true hard porcelain. Marks are much more frequent than on English pieces, but have to be treated with suspicion as they stayed in use over long periods and were copied freely. The supremacy of Dresden induced many makers, on the Continent as well as in England, to mark their wares with the crossed swords or with the *AR* monogram.

Just as in England there were 'outside decorators', in Germany and Austria there were 'Hausmalers' (literally, *home painters*), who bought unpainted ware and decorated it themselves in their own individual styles. Many of these men were excellent artists and did work of high quality, but they were not popular with the factories. At Dresden, all pieces sold in the white after about 1760 had one or more short lines cut through the crossed swords to indicate that they were imperfect. While many of the imperfections were only slight, they were sufficient to make the ware unfit for decorating by the factory painters.

It should be remembered that many Continental factories are still in production and re-use eighteenth-century moulds of their own and other makers' wares. Often they mark them appropriately, and it is far from easy for the novice to distinguish between old and new. Careful examination of genuine pieces and a comparison of them with modern copies, are the only ways to recognize and learn the difference. It may comfort the puzzled beginner to know that fifty years ago a director of the Sèvres factory confessed he was completely unable to distinguish old from new when some doubtful pieces from the Victoria and Albert Museum were submitted for his opinion.

CONTINENTAL PORCELAIN FACTORIES

GERMANY

Dresden (Saxony), East Germany

In the year 1707, Johann Böttger, an alchemist, was investigating the possibility of making gold, when his services were enlisted to discover what seemed at the time an equally insoluble secret: how to make porcelain to rival the Oriental ware then being imported into Europe in quantity. As a result of his successful experiments in making a hard red ware, he was able to make a white one, and on 23rd January 1710 the Royal Saxon Manufactory was established. It was in an old fortress at Meissen, near Dresden in Saxony, and there it remained for nearly 150 years. The porcelain produced since 1710 is called Meissen in Germany and the United States, Dresden in England, and Saxe in France, and was the first to be made in Europe in the Oriental manner from a fused mixture of minerals.

From the start, both the red and the white wares were made in quantity, but examples of them are very rare today. The former were often decorated on the lapidary's wheel, the polished parts appearing as if glazed. A few figures were made, but the output was principally cups and bowls, and many of these in white porcelain had coloured decoration.

Böttger died in 1719, and from then onwards there were numerous changes in both personnel and output, culminating in the appointment of Johann Kändler as modeller in 1731. It was Kändler's creation of dozens of brilliant figures and groups that spread the fame of Meissen throughout Europe, and inspired modellers of every nation.

As well as figures, Dresden made tablewares, and initiated a series of tureens and covered pots in the form of animals, fishes, birds, flowers, fruit and vegetables. Proof of the success of all these is the fact that so many factories, at one time or another, imitated not only the designs but also added a fake crossed-swords mark. The latter often on wares far removed from anything likely to have come from Germany, but taking full advantage of the high reputation that country enjoyed for making fine china.

Design and workmanship reached their heights in the years between 1740 and 1750; the years during which most countries were managing to start their own soft-paste factories in attempts to rival the imported product. It was the decade that saw the fashion for porcelain as a dinner-table decoration; temples, fountains and palaces were made to stand in the centre of the board, surrounded by the inhabitants of a world of fantasy created by the potter. The banquets of Continental royalties stimulated the production of these pieces, but the custom does not seem to have been widespread in England.

The Seven Years War from 1756 to 1763 saw the end of the most important and prolific period of Dresden, and although new models were introduced continuously afterwards none capture the brilliance of the earlier years. Kändler died in 1775, when the factory was under the direction of Count Camillo Marcolini; whose name is given to the period 1774 to 1814, when he was the government minister responsible for the factory.

Dresden china was copied not only in the countries where it was imported but the factory re-issued the same models again and again. The composition of the body and glaze has changed little, but new colours have been introduced from time to time. It is these, together with the quality of painting and the finish of the porcelain, that distinguish old from new.

From the year 1713, when examples of Dresden white porcelain were exhibited at the Leipzig Easter Fair, a bid was made to capture markets throughout Europe. Saxony badly needed money, which was why Böttger had been endeavouring in the first place to make gold, and the export of porcelain was to be the means of providing it. The policy was successful until the Seven Years War upset progress, but by that date almost every country had its own manufactories, and once the German works had loosed its grip it was never regained.

It was due to the activities of a small number of Arcanists, men who knew or professed to know the secrets of porcelain-manufacture, that other factories came into being following the success of Dresden. These men offered their knowledge and services where they thought it would pay them best, and in spite of the strictest precautions to prevent their defection. The first to benefit was Vienna in Austria.

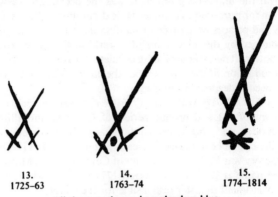

| 13. | 14. | 15. |
| 1725–63 | 1763–74 | 1774–1814 |

All these marks are in underglaze blue.

Other factories in Germany were founded about the middle of the eighteenth century and each produced hard-paste wares of varying quality and interest. They include:

Höchst, near Frankfort (West Germany)

The best-known figures are a series of children which are very carefully modelled and painted, and have been copied during the past hundred years in both porcelain and pottery. The factory mark, which has also been imitated, is a spoked wheel in blue or red.

Berlin

A wool-merchant named Wilhelm Wegely started a factory in 1752 but it was unsuccessful and closed five years later. In 1761 a further factory was opened by a financier named Gotzkowsky, it was bought by the King of Prussia, Frederick the Great, in 1763. Wares similar to, and in imitation of, Dresden were made but the china is colder in appearance and the colourings tend to be more vivid. In the nineteenth century the factory made copies of oil paintings in miniature on flat slabs of the ware, and also made lithophanes. These are panels of biscuit-ware stamped in intaglio so that they appear in light and shade when held against a window or light. The mark commonly found is a sceptre in underglaze blue, with or without the letters 'K.P.M.'.

Fürstenburg, near Cassel (West Germany)

This factory was started in 1753, and after initial difficulties produced good quality wares of all types in the Dresden manner. Some outstanding figures were modelled by Simon Feilner, who had worked at Höchst, and a unique set of fifteen of these was sold in London in July 1960, for £15,000. The factory is still in operation. The mark is a script letter 'F' in blue, on modern pieces it has a crown above.

Nymphenburg, near Munich (West Germany)

Although all types of wares were made at this Bavarian factory, its name is linked with that of the Swiss-born modeller, Franz Anton Bustelli, who created a number of superb figures. Of all porcelain figures, English or Continental in origin, these, possessing both grace and action and with their soft and careful colouring are surely the most exciting and satisfying made anywhere. Bustelli's figures were made in the first instance between 1754 and 1763, but the moulds were re-used by the factory at a later date. The Nymphenburg works is still in operation. The principal mark is an impressed shield with diamond-shaped checks.

Ludwigsburg, near Stuttgart

The porcelain made at Ludwigsburg from 1758 was not of a white colour, but tended to a smoky brown in tone. Figures were a large proportion of the output, and these included a series of miniature groups, some of market-stalls with their wares and attendants, and some attractive figures of dancers. The factory closed in 1824. The mark comprises two letter 'c's back to back, sometimes with a crown above, in blue.

There were a number of other factories of varying importance, each copying Dresden and one another, and occasionally producing original work of above-average quality. Some of them used their own marks, some used imitations of Dresden, but most of them marked only a few of their productions and there are large numbers of unmarked pieces which it is difficult or impossible to allocate to any particular factory.

AUSTRIA

Vienna

In 1719, with the help of a runaway from Dresden, a factory was started under the managership of Claud du Pacquier. It made fine hard-paste porcelain resembling Dresden in paste more than in design or colouring. Du Pacquier's factory faced continual difficulties; ware was costly to produce and much of it too dear to find many purchasers. It is rare today. In 1744 the factory was bought by the Austrian State and successful efforts were made to popularize its products. This porcelain, known

16. In underglaze blue.
1749–1820, but used
again later.

from its mark of a shield in blue, finally evolved an individual style of heavily gilded pieces painted carefully in the manner of miniatures. These were first made towards the end of the eighteenth century, but were copied again and again until the factory closed in 1864. Some of the modern and very garish imitations of this type of Vienna porcelain bears the printed 'signature' of the artist; often that of the English painter, Angelica Kauffmann.

FRANCE

Saint-Cloud

Soft-paste porcelain is said to have been made at Rouen as early as 1673, but although several specimens have been brought forward as proof of the statement they are not accepted generally as having been made there. The earliest accepted pieces are those made at Saint-Cloud at the end of the seventeenth century. They are mostly of a creamy colour, but occasionally of a bluish white, and all kinds of wares were made. Painting was in underglaze blue and in colours, and much was in the popular Oriental manner. Examples of the ware are not commonly found, and figures, of which few were made, are the rarest. The most common mark is $^{St.}_{T}C$ in blue or incised. The factory closed in 1766.

Chantilly

A soft-paste factory was founded at Chantilly in 1725 and made wares covered in an attractive glaze containing tin which gave it a smooth, white, and distinctive appearance. Tablewares, vases and other useful pieces were made, and neatly decorated in brilliant colours that rely on the beautiful white surface for their full effect. Later wares were lead-glazed and of a creamy colour, and one of the last patterns introduced was widely copied; a small spray of cornflowers known as the 'Chantilly sprig'. After being owned for a few years by an Englishman named Potter the factory closed in 1800. The mark is a curved hunting-horn in red or blue.

Mennecy

The factory best known by the name of Mennecy was started in 1734 in Paris, fourteen years later moved outside the capital to Mennecy, and in 1773 moved finally to Bourg-la-Reine. The early wares are usually of a milky-white colour, with a 'wet-looking' glaze and a slightly undulating surface; in very rare instances a tin-glaze, in imitation of that used at Chantilly, is found. All types of wares, including a number of figures and groups, were painted in colours and many show a particularly striking use of pink and bright blue. The mark comprises the letters 'D V', incised or in blue.

Sèvres

The National Manufactory of porcelain in France was started in a disused château in the suburbs of Paris in 1738. In that year some workmen who had left the Chantilly factory and claimed to know the secrets of making porcelain, were engaged to conduct experiments to that end. They failed to make good their boasts and are said to have spent most of their time drinking, with the result that they were sent away in disgrace and another arcanist employed in their place. Finally, in 1745, success was achieved, and Royal permission given to form a company to make 'porcelain in the style of the Saxon, that is to say, painted and gilded with human figures'.

Undoubtedly the factory aimed at challenging the hold that Germany had on the French market, and replacing the imported wares by home-produced ones. From the start the best chemists, goldsmiths and other experts were employed, and decrees were passed forbidding any other factory in France from making porcelain or the workmen at the new factory to leave and reveal the secrets. By 1750 more than a hundred workers were employed, and three years later a further order again prohibited manufacture by any rival concern; an order that does not seem to have been taken very seriously. In 1753, also, it was proposed to build new premises at Sèvres, again close to Paris and on the way to Versailles, and when the erection was completed in 1756 the move was made. After a number of financial difficulties, growing pains common to the porcelain factories of all nations, the establishment was taken over by Louis XV in 1760.

The justly-famous Sèvres soft-paste porcelain quickly rose to a high position as a leader of fashion, and when the Seven Years'

War started in 1756, the French factory was able to leap ahead as its rival fell into the hands of Frederick the Great and the Prussian soldiers. A large part of the early output was devoted to the making of artificial flowers of all kinds that were coloured naturally. On one occasion Madame de Pompadour received the King in a conservatory filled with quantities of these porcelain blooms which were perfumed to make them more convincing.

Figures began to be made at an early date, and the majority were glazed and uncoloured. In 1751 came the introduction of figures made and sold in the biscuit; an entirely new idea that was very successful and that employed many first-class modellers.

The magnificent vases made at Sèvres were finely painted in panels on grounds of colours that were envied and copied throughout Europe: dark blue, turquoise, yellow, green, and rose-pink (known as *Rose du Barry* or *Rose Pompadour*). Many of the vases were made especially for presentation by the King to foreign Royalties and acted as excellent ambassadors of trade; orders flowed to the factory in their wake.

In spite of the success and popularity of the Sèvres soft-paste the directors of the manufactory were not satisfied and continued to attempt to make hard-paste: 'in the style of the Saxon.' Eventually, they succeeded, and by 1772, the new material was being manufactured in quantity.

The use of hard-paste enabled much larger pieces to be made, and lowered the proportion of losses in firing, but the ware lost much of its beauty as a result. In the nineteenth century numbers of large vases and covers were made, many painted with pseudo-eighteenth-century scenes on a turquoise ground and heavily mounted in gilt metal. Services painted with portraits of Royal and noble personages were also popular.

About 1800, following the Revolution, changes in direction and policy caused the sale of great quantities of 'seconds' and stored undecorated pieces, that were bought by English and French 'outside decorators'. These genuinely old soft-paste specimens were carefully painted in authentic styles and colours; also, sparsely-decorated old Sèvres has sometimes had its enamelling removed with acid and more valuable embellishment added and glazed. At Coalport and elsewhere in England, and at some Continental factories, clever forgeries were made. Altogether, the collector should bear in mind the words of W. B. Honey: 'It is probable that more than half the porcelain purporting to be Sèvres in private hands is partly or wholly false.'

The mark, which is often imitated, comprises two script 'L's facing each other and interlinked. There is often an additional letter between them to denote the year of manufacture.

Paris

Although the French factories mentioned above were situated in or near the city of Paris, there were a number of small ones in addition making hard-paste wares that are known generally as 'Paris Porcelain'. These were all started after about 1770, and some twenty or so different makers came and went between that date and 1830. Straight-sided coffee-cups, with saucers, are frequently found and have neatly painted coloured decoration and gilding. Some of the pieces are marked with the name of the factory stencilled in red, but much is unmarked.

Jacob Petit

A further hard-paste factory was at Fontainebleau, just outside Paris, and this was bought in 1830 by two brothers, Jacob and Mardochée Petit. They made a great quantity of wares of all kinds, brightly painted and heavily gilt, heavily modelled but decorative in appearance. Clock cases and vases are found commonly, and many bear the initials of Jacob Petit, by whose name the porcelain is known, in underglaze blue.

Eastern France

Several factories were started in the east of France, close to the frontier with Germany. None lasted for any considerable time and, on the whole, their productions are not distinguished. At Strasburg both tablewares and figures were made, and although some of the latter are copied from Sèvres models others are original.

Porcelain was made at Niderviller from 1765, and all types of wares were made including some good figures in white biscuit. An unusual style of decorating porcelain practised there achieved some popularity, and consisted of a *trompe l'oeil*. This took the form of an engraving of a landscape pinned to a piece of wood with well-defined grain, painted carefully on the china in natural colours. Good biscuit figures were made also at Lunéville.

ITALY

Florence

During the fifteenth and sixteenth centuries much experimental work was carried on in attempts to imitate Chinese porcelain, which had been brought to Europe by then. Documents record that some of the Venetian glass-makers were making trials, but it is believed that they resulted in only a white glass. Of this Venetian ware a few specimens have survived, and are the subject of continual argument.

By 1575 a method of making soft-paste porcelain had been found in Florence, under the patronage of Francesco Maria de' Medici, Grand Duke of Tuscany, and this is known in consequence as 'Medici Porcelain'. Of the pieces made between the years 1575 and 1587, when the works apparently closed, it has been calculated that fifty-nine survive. Of these, forty-one are now in museums, four are in private possession and fourteen have disappeared over the years. A plate that had been lost, was rediscovered and sold in London in 1949 for £1,100. It is now in an American museum. It may be added that, inevitably, a few forgeries have been found.

Almost all the surviving located Medici porcelain is painted in underglaze blue, and occasionally with additional outlining in dark purple. The mark is usually a large-scale drawing in blue of the dome of Sta. Maria del Fiore, the Cathedral of Florence.

Venice

The first factory here was started in 1720 by Francesco Vezzi, it made a hard-paste porcelain varying in colour from grey to white, but encountered financial difficulties and was closed by 1740 or earlier. Tablewares were made, and cups, saucers and teapots are the principal survivors. Most pieces are marked with the name of the city 'Venezia' or the abbreviations 'Vena' or 'Va'. The practice of marking the output simplifies identification, but the mark has been added sometimes to pieces from other factories.

The next factory was opened by two dealers in Dresden china, Maria and Nathaniel Hewelcke. Their venture began in 1758, but lasted for only five years. A condition of being allowed to start a factory was that all their wares must be marked with a letter 'v'; which is found incised in the clay and painted red.

The most successful Venice factory was that directed by Geminiano Cozzi, a banker, who opened it in 1764. The hard-paste material was greyish in colour, and all types of wares, including figures, were made. The factory closed in 1812, after many years during which a high output was achieved. Figures and groups rarely have a mark, but other pieces are painted with an anchor in red; usually of a large size, and not to be confused with the very small red one used at an earlier date at Chelsea.

At Le Nove, near Bassano, about twenty-five miles north-west of Venice a factory was opened in 1752 by Pasquale Antonibon, who already made majolica there. After numerous vicissitudes including defaulting workmen, it closed finally in 1835. The wares produced were of all kinds and the paste resembled closely that of Cozzi's factory; grey in colour 'with a wet-looking glaze that develops a brownish tone where it lies thick'. The mark used was a six-pointed star, drawn with three short intersecting lines, or the word 'NOVE' incised or in relief.

Doccia, *near Florence*

This factory was started by the Marchese Carlo Ginori in 1735, remained in the ownership of his descendants until 1896, and is still in production. The factory has made all types of wares, many of which are notable for their exuberant modelling and decoration. A series of tablewares moulded in low relief with mythological scenes, coloured and with the flesh tones rendered

9. *Above:* English glass: decanter with cut decoration, 1820; wine glass diamond-engraved in Holland with a coat-of-arms, 1775; sealed wine bottle dated 1698; wine glass with opaque twist stem and enamelled bowl, 1750; goblet, the stem containing a silver coin of 1684.

10. *Below:* Early nineteenth-century English porcelain: Rockingham 'cottage' pastille-burner; Nantgarw plate painted with roses; Chamberlain's Worcester sugar basin and cover; Derby figure of Africa.

11. *Above:* English eighteenth-century pottery: Nottingham brown salt-glaze tankard, 1710; Staffordshire saltglaze 'brick' for holding flowers with blue decoration, 1760; Wedgwood tankard with silver rim, 1780.

12. *Below:* Continental pottery: Hamburg wine bottle dated 1657; Marseilles plate painted with flowers, 1770; Bayreuth plate, 1760; Venetian drug jar (Albarello), late seventeenth century.

13. *Below:* English porcelain of the eighteenth century: Chelsea plate, gold anchor mark; Worcester tankard with transfer-printed design; Chelsea 'goat and bee' jug, triangle mark; Lund's Worcester cream jug; Dr. Wall period Worcester oval spoon tray (part of a teaset, and on which spoons were brought to the table); Liverpool cream jug painted with Oriental figures; Lowestoft cream jug painted with flowers; Longton Hall plate, the border patterned with strawberry leaves.

14. *Above, left:* American silver candlestick by Cornelius Kierstede, *c.* 1705.

15. *Above, right:* American silver tankard by Gerrit Onckelbag, 1670–1732.

16. *Below:* American silver by Paul Revere, Jr. Teapot, 1796, bowl, 1790; jug, 1790–1800, from another set.

17. *Above:* Sheffield plate of the late eighteenth century: candlestick, sauce tureen and cover, teapot stand, and sweetmeat dish.

18. *Below:* English delft pottery: candlestick, 1650; dish commemorating the coronation of William and Mary, 1689; dish painted with Adam and Eve and with 'blue dash' border, 1650; plate dated 1750; tankard painted with the arms of the Blacksmiths' Company, and dated 1752.

by stippling was introduced as early as about 1760, and re-issued continuously. Through misunderstandings, and as a trade 'trick', the nineteenth-century versions were sold as products of the Capodimonte factory, and this name has stuck to them quite wrongly for fully a century. The Doccia paste is of a grey colour and often shows fire-cracks, the surface is rough and the glaze appears less shiny than many. The mark on eighteenth-century pieces is a star, taken from the arms of the Ginori family, more solid in the centre than the same mark used at Le Nove. The nineteenth-century Doccia copies of earlier wares, known as 'Capodimonte', have a crowned 'N' in underglaze blue or impressed. Imitations of these copies have, in turn, been made in Germany and France, and some of these are marked similarly.

Capodimonte, near Naples

The King of Naples married a daughter of Augustus the Strong, King of Saxony, who owned the Meissen factory and gave his daughter seventeen table services as part of her dowry. It is not surprising to learn that her husband became anxious to make porcelain in his own country; he succeeded in 1743 and a factory was opened in the grounds of the palace of Capodimonte. Sixteen years later, the King of Naples became Charles III of Spain, and removed most of the workmen and equipment to the garden of his palace of Buen Retiro in Madrid. The buildings were fortified by the French during the Peninsular War, and destroyed by Wellington's troops in 1812.

The Capodimonte ware is made of a creamy white soft-paste, of which surviving examples are usually finely decorated. Figures are rarely seen outside museums; many of them are original models comparable with the best of the eighteenth century. Some of the Capodimonte composition was shipped to Spain when the move was made to Buen Retiro, but this was expensive and attempts were made to find local substitutes. Eventually a good white paste was made, but on the whole the work produced in Spain is not considered to compare either in material or modelling with that done in Italy. In its earlier days the factory made snuff-boxes and other pieces modelled with naturalistic sea shells, and tablewares were often painted with scenes of horsemen at battle. The same marks were used at both factories: a fleur-delys in blue or gold, or incised.

Naples

The son of Charles of Spain, Ferdinand IV, King of Naples, started in 1771 a manufactory in emulation of that formerly at Capodimonte. A creamy white soft-paste was used for figures and tablewares, and figures were made in the fashionable biscuit. Some extensive table services were produced for presentation for diplomatic purposes; one sent to George III in 1787 is preserved at Windsor Castle.

The marks are: the letters 'RF' in blue with a crown above; and a crowned 'N' in red or blue or impressed.

BELGIUM

Tournay

A good soft-paste porcelain was made here from about 1751; at first it was greyish in appearance, but later it became a good creamy white. Both the Sèvres and Meissen styles were copied, but much original work was done in both tablewares and figures. A quantity of tableware with painting in underglaze blue is similar in appearance to Worcester, and some of the groups are akin to those of Chelsea. This is not surprising in view of the fact that some ex-Tournay craftsmen actually worked at Chelsea for a time, but it does not excuse the occasional modern practice of adding anchors and triangles to genuine Tournay groups! Painting was often of excellent quality, and a series of plates painted with animals within dark blue and gilt borders compare well with Sèvres. Some Tournay porcelain was sold to the Hague factory and decorated there.

During the nineteenth century much forging of eighteenth-century English and French soft-paste porcelains was carried on at Tournay, and they also reissued some of their own models of earlier date.

Genuine marks in colours or gold are a roughly-drawn tower, or a version of the Dresden crossed swords but with a small cross at each opening.

HOLLAND

Weesp, near Amsterdam

A hard-paste manufactory was started in 1759, some of the workers were Germans thrown out of employment by the Seven Years War so German styles predominated as regards models and painting. The mark, also, was a version of the Dresden crossed swords but with three dots placed about them. In 1771 the factory was bought by Johannes de Mol and removed to Oude Loosdrecht; a similar paste was used, and the mark was changed to the letters 'M.O.L.' incised or painted in colour. A further move followed in 1784 to Amstel and the mark then became the name of that place in black or blue. Popular products of these factories were sets of vases elaborately pierced and sparsely decorated, but with the little painting on them of good quality.

The Hague

A decorating establishment bought unpainted wares from various factories and decorated them, adding a mark in blue of a stork with a fish in its beak. Porcelain was made on the premises from about 1776 until 1790 and has the same mark.

SWITZERLAND

Zurich

A factory was opened in 1763 and started by making a creamy white soft-paste which is now very rare. Two years later, hardpaste was made and this was decorated very carefully in distinctive styles that make the ware some of the most beautiful of its period. Figures are rare, expensive, and many are very attractively modelled and coloured. Little or no porcelain was made after about 1791. The mark is the letter 'z' in underglaze blue, sometimes with one or more dots below.

Nyon, near Geneva

This factory, starting in 1780, made a good hard-paste. Tablewares were the principal productions, and the few figures are very rare. The mark is a fish in outline, but it should be noted that a mark resembling this was used elsewhere.

SCANDINAVIA

Marieberg, near Stockholm, Sweden

A soft-paste was made here from 1766 to 1769, it is a cream-tinted glassy ware and small vases, custard cups and other pieces were made from it. A different paste was later introduced, followed for a short time by a hard-paste. Some figures were made, and more custard cups and mustard pots. The mark is usually a monogram of 'M' and 'B' sometimes with three small crowns above.

Copenhagen

A soft-paste factory operated from 1759 to 1765, but its productions are very rare. The hard-paste Royal factory began about 1771 and is still in production. Tableware, much of it decorated in underglaze blue, was made, and also many figures. The mark is three wavy lines one over the other, in underglaze blue.

RUSSIA

The Imperial factory at St Petersburg (now Leningrad) did not begin production until about 1758 and few of the products of its early years are to be seen outside Russia. Large vases were made in the early nineteenth century and some were given as presents to ambassadors and others; they compare well with the work of European factories. Figures and groups of Russian workers and peasants were made, and these are sometimes to be seen. Several factories were in existence in Moscow at the end of the eighteenth century and in the first quarter of the nineteenth: they produced similar pieces to the Imperial establishment.

CHAPTER FOURTEEN

Oriental pottery and porcelain

ORIENTAL pottery and procelain was made principally in China, Korea and Japan. The wares made in these countries, and in those bordering on the first two, resemble each other superficially, and both beginner and expert suffer confusion. A proportion of the old wares was marked, usually under the base of the article and in underglaze blue, but just as the shapes and colours of earlier periods were imitated in succeeding centuries, so were the marks.

CHINA

Many people talk about, and others wonder about, the dynasties and emperors of old China. It is as well, therefore, to preface this section with a list of those most likely to be of use:

Dynasties		*Emperors*	
Chou	About 1122 to 249 B.C.		
Han	206 B.C. to A.D. 220		
T'ang	618 to A.D. 906		
Sung	960 to 1279		
Ming	1368 to 1644	Hsüan Tê	1426 to 1435
		Ch'êng Hua	1465 to 1487
		Wan Li	1573 to 1619
Ch'ing	1644 to 1912	K'ang Hsi	1662 to 1722
		Yung Chêng	1723 to 1735
		Ch'ien Lung	1736 to 1795
		Chia Ch'ing	1796 to 1820
		Tao Kuang	1821 to 1850

From before 200 B.C. little pottery has survived. The custom of burying pottery vessels and figures with the body of a dead

103

person, and the reopening of undisturbed tombs, has enabled students to gain an idea of the wares of the Han dynasty. These mortuary pieces show that a green glaze containing lead was commonly in use, and that decoration, where present, consisted of painting in unfired colours, or of attractive incised patterns. It is argued that the tomb wares, intended for the use of the deceased in a future life, were made perfunctorily, and that the hitherto-unidentified domestic pieces must have been of better workmanship and of a higher artistic quality.

Then followed a gap of four centuries during which no appreciable advances were made, but the years lost in strife and artistic stagnation were amply made up for by the brilliance of the T'ang dynasty. The large tomb figures of horses and camels, splashed with glazes of orange-brown and green, are among the best-known objects made at the time. Time and interment have given the glaze a silvery iridescence that lends an added attraction. Dishes and other pieces of the period are less familiar to many, but are artistically important in many instances. Stoneware was brought a stage further forward by giving it a white body, and the pieces known as Yüeh (abbreviated from Yüeh Chou, a district in Chekiang province where they were made) with their fine celadon glaze, were produced.

In the succeeding Sung dynasty, many further styles were introduced and older ones developed. Carved and incised designs are found, and pale-coloured glazes of great beauty were used alongside the popular celadon green which is found on pieces exported to the Near East countries. All these delicately modelled and coloured wares were copied in later Ming times, but apart from differences in finishing, the early pieces were made of a stoneware and the later of true porcelain.

The coming of the Ming dynasty saw the emergence of Ching-tê-chên, to the south-west of Nankin, as a centre of manufacture. Here, in the fourteenth century, was organized the series of factories making the porcelain that spread the fame of China throughout the civilized world. The rare pieces decorated in underglaze blue of the reigns of Hsüan Tê and Ch'êng Hua are the forerunners of the vast quantities later made for export to the West, and of which examples are still relatively commonplace. Another esteemed type are the 'three-colour' wares, usually in the form of vases, with the design outlined in raised threads of clay and filled with coloured glazes. These latter date from the reign of Wan Li, when the combination of underglaze blue, and overglaze red, yellow, green and aubergine (brown-purple) was used with effect; a style that led to the well-known *famille verte* of the reign of K'ang Hsi. A smaller factory at Tê-hua, in the south of China, was producing the fine white ware, known as blanc-de-chine (Chinese white), which it continued to copy continually in succeeding centuries.

By this date, about 1600, exportation to Europe was beginning to take place, although 'blue and white' (or Nankin, as it is often called) probably formed the bulk. It was towards the end of the seventeenth century, in the reign of the emperor K'ang Hsi, that this export trade assumed enormous proportions and the types of porcelain with which Europeans are familiar were made in quantity. The most popular is the so-called *famille verte* (green family) with its predominating bright greens and red. All manner of articles were decorated in this style, from sets of vases to figures of goddesses. Large vases were sometimes painted in other colour-combinations: *famille jaune* and *famille noire*, in which the ground colour was yellow and black respectively. Examples of these were never numerous, and are now extremely rare.

The single-colour (monochrome) glazes and enamels produced in the Ming dynasty were not only copied, but extended in range during the eighteenth century. A variety of reds and browns was developed, and some of these were controlled skilfully in the kiln to produce unusual effects. Other colours, including yellows and greens, were devised, and a rich ruby red was used sometimes on a class of wares made for export. It occurs on the backs of thin 'eggshell' plates of the Yung Chêng period, and as a ground colour on vases and dishes of the same date. A further innovation in combination with panels of *famille verte* was the appropriately named 'powder-blue'. This was made by blowing

powdered cobalt through a gauze screen, the panels being pro-
tected by pieces of paper, the resulting powdered ground vibrat-
ing with colour under the smooth glaze in the best examples.
Pieces were sometimes enveloped entirely in powder-blue, and
decorated over the glaze with designs in the thin and dull gilding
used by the Chinese.

By this time, Jesuit missionaries from France had established
themselves in China, and were sending back notes of what they
could learn of the processes of porcelain making. Of these men,
Père d'Entrecolles was the most successful and his letters, when
they were published eventually, had a great effect on the art in
Europe. In the reverse direction, Europeans of all the nations
then established in trade with China, were sending to their
agents in the East pieces of silver, pottery and other articles to
have them imitated in the wonder material; at the same time,
they sent engravings and drawings to be copied as decoration.
These tasks were performed by the Chinese with great skill, and
resulted in a constant flood of goods in both directions throughout the eighteenth century.

A further stimulus to the trade was public interest in tea-
drinking, and the sending of increasing amounts of the leaf
from China. The beverage being new to the West, no drinking-
vessels entirely suitable were available, and the Orientals oblig-
ingly sent porcelain cups and saucers and teapots. Many of these
travelled packed in the holds of East Indiamen with the tea
above, so that the bilge-water would not ruin the latter.

The first teapots sent from the East were made of a hard red
stoneware, known as Yi-hsing pottery, and the legend quickly
grew that tea could only be enjoyed if poured from a red pot.
It will be found that many of the first teapots made in Europe
(other than those of silver) were of red stoneware in imitation of
the imported ones.

With the discoveries of Böttger and the making of porcelain in
Europe, the Chinese monopoly was broken, but the novelty of
having something from far Cathay was sufficient to ensure a
market. In addition, the Chinese wares, in spite of the expenses

of packing and transport, were cheaper than European-made ones. One early effect of European research was that just as the Chinese had copied the cobalt blue of the Persians, so they imitated the pink colour used successfully at Dresden. In the reign of Yung Chêng this was employed extensively, and completely changed the prevailing tone of decorated porcelain. The opaque pink gave its name to the type of colouring: *famille rose*, which lasted for the rest of the eighteenth century through the reign of Ch'ien Lung.

The transmission of designs continued, and one popular feature was the ordering of complete dinner services painted with the coat-of-arms, crest or initials of the European owner. Punch-bowls, mugs, teasets, and innumerable other articles were ornamented in a similar manner and are sought eagerly today. About 1800, America was also importing from China, and there remain in the United States many examples of old porcelain with the insignia of their former owners. An outstanding punch-bowl given to the City of New York in 1802 bears a view of the city, and is inscribed with the date of presentation as well as the name of the Chinese artist who painted it.

By many people on both sides of the Atlantic much of this eighteenth-century porcelain exported from China is called 'Lowestoft'. It was given this name mistakenly a century ago, and although the error was corrected soon afterwards the name has stayed.

Although a large quantity of old Chinese porcelain was made for export, there was a certain amount for the supply of the home market. In many instances this was made to much higher standards in both modelling and painting, and was generally very carefully finished. On the whole, it was sparsely decorated and relied as much on the beauty of the shape and surface of the ware as on the actual brushwork. This ware, known as being in the 'Chinese taste', is rarely found out of China but is sought eagerly by collectors.

With the advent of the nineteenth century, the eighteenth-century styles continued but the quality of both painting and porcelain fell off. In the Tao Kuang period was introduced the manner of painting the entire surface of a piece with flowers and butterflies against a green ground; this is known generally as 'Canton' ware.

The Chinese have always been careful copyists, and their work in porcelain is no exception. It has been mentioned that Yüeh ware of the T'ang dynasty was copied in the Ming period, but the same process has been continued down to modern times. Twentieth-century imitations of K'ang Hsi are often convincingly done and only experienced collectors can tell them from the originals. Equally, the clever reproductions of Samson of Paris and of the Herend factory in Austria must be guarded against.

Chinese porcelain is a life-time study, and a fascinating one. New discoveries are being made continually, new theories brought forward, and the wares have an unequalled international interest. There is no short cut in learning how to differentiate between old and new: experience gained from handling and studying pieces is the only way. Although copies of early examples may seem convincing, a careful examination will reveal that subtleties in shaping and colour have been lost, and the collector must aim to discern this at a glance.

KOREA

Korea is situated to the north of China, and is a peninsula adjoining Manchuria and pointing south towards Japan. The pottery and porcelain made there has strong characteristics of its own both in shape and decoration. The finest wares were made in the Koryu period which lasted from A.D. 936 to 1392, and was roughly contemporary with the Sung period in China. In the following Yi period, the making of many of the earlier types of wares continued.

The most typical Koryu pieces are of a hard stoneware with a celadon glaze. Decoration took various forms: incising under the glaze is common, but the most interesting is the use of inlay. The pattern was cut into the article with a tool, and the incisions filled with black or white clay. The Koreans were very skilled at this work, and it is possible that they were the first to perfect it.

Distinctive features of many of the Korean celadons are that where the bare clay is exposed it shows a red colour, and usually the low footring and convex base is glazed all over. Most bases show also three or more small marks where they have stood on 'stilts' in the kiln; the 'stilts' being used to prevent the melted glaze from sticking to the floor or to any other piece being fired.

To many Western eyes Korean wares have a refreshing and attractive character that reveals no trace at all of the European influences so common in Chinese pieces. Apart from the celadons, little is known about other types of ware found in both Korea and China, and which may have originated in either country.

JAPAN

The majority of Japanese porcelain to be seen outside that country is ware that was made purposely for export. Little, if any, porcelain at all was made there before the sixteenth century, but by the seventeenth century kilns were in operation near Arita, in the province of Hizen.

Probably the best-known wares, apart from nineteenth-century Satsuma, are the dishes and jars decorated in the so-called 'Imari' style, from the name of the port near Arita whence they were brought to Europe by Dutch traders. This Imari porcelain is painted on a heavy bluish-toned body with a mixture of flowers, scrolls and panels in dark blue, red and gold. At the time it was brought to the West it was highly esteemed, and although it has been copied extensively (Crown Derby is a familiar example) it is less popular today.

The other Japanese ware that had an influence on Western porcelain is that known as 'Kakiemon', after Sakaida Kakiemon, one of a family of Arita potters. Pieces with this style of decoration derived from the Chinese, are sparsely painted in red, green, blue, turquoise and yellow, and they were copied closely at Dresden, Chantilly, Chelsea and elsewhere.

Some of the Japanese potters imitated closely current Chinese wares, and these are easily confused. Many Japanese pieces have small marks under the bases where they stood on clay 'stilts' when being fired. Many, also, show a reddish-orange colour on the unglazed edges.

Other porcelains and styles of decoration were current in Japan at the time that these export pieces were being made, but comparatively few specimens have left the country.

BOOKS

There are many books dealing with individual pottery and porcelain factories, but the best general works are:

European: *European Ceramic Art*, by W. B. Honey, published in 1952. It is a large thick volume (with a thinner supplementary volume of illustrations) containing 'a dictionary of factories, artists, technical terms, and general information', and reproduces a large number of marks. Also, it contains full bibliographies up to 1952 relating to each factory.

Oriental: *The Ceramic Art of China*, by W. B. Honey, published in 1945. This contains also chapters dealing with the wares of Indo-China, Korea and Japan, and is well illustrated.

Marks are reproduced in *Handbook of Pottery & Porcelain Marks*, by J. P. Cushion and W. B. Honey, and in *The Collector's Handbook of Marks and Monograms on Pottery and Porcelain*, by William Chaffers.

Part III

GLASS, SILVER, PLATE, ENAMELS, METALWORK

CHAPTER FIFTEEN

Glass

OF ancient glass probably the best-known example in the world is the Portland Vase in the British Museum; this is composed of a layer of white glass over blue glass, the outer coating skilfully cut into a pattern. More ordinary types of glass dating to Roman times are in the form of small bottles, often called 'Tear Bottles', which have been excavated and as a result of lengthy burial are covered in iridescence. The Romans mastered the art of making glass of all the types known in later years, and subsequent techniques have been rediscoveries. Considering the centuries that have passed and the delicacy of the material a considerable number of fine specimens has survived, but they are to be seen rarely outside museums.

Following the fall of the Roman Empire, the art of glass-making suffered a decline, but in Persia and other countries of the Near East some good pieces were made between the seventh and eleventh centuries. Later, in Syria some highly decorated articles, notably vases and mosque-lamps, were made and specimens of these outstanding works may be seen in the principal museums. At the same time, in Europe low bowls and cups were being made from a greenish or brownish coloured glass. A peculiarity of these is that the fitting of a foot to the articles, common enough in Roman times, seldom seems to occur; it would appear that the arts of making a foot and joining it to a vessel had been forgotten.

111

Venice

By the thirteenth century glass-making had become a well-established industry in Venice and on the island of Murano, where a large and important export trade was built up rapidly. The Venetians had found how to make a clear glass, *cristallo*, and were able to produce not only colourless pieces but others of pure gem-like tints. These various types of glass and the skill with which they were fashioned ensured a ready sale, and gave Venice an enduring fame. One of the techniques rediscovered shortly before 1650, lost since Egyptian and Roman times, was the embedding in clear glass of threads of white or coloured glass, the former known as *latticino*; dishes, and other pieces were made with lace-like patterns of mathematical precision. Other types of decoration were with enamels painted on the surface and fired (similar to the painting of chinaware), gilding, and engraving. The white glass used in the making of latticino pieces was used sometimes to make complete pieces; their resemblance to porcelain was recognized and often led to confusion. It is recorded that about 1470 a white glass was the subject of experiments to imitate Chinese porcelain, and as late as 1730 the French scientist, Réaumur, was working on much the same lines.

The Venetian trade declined once the spread of knowledge had enabled glass-works to be set up in other countries, but production continued. Both coloured and white glass were made throughout the eighteenth century and later, and chandeliers were introduced. These were often of large size, made of opaque glass tinted in pinks and blues and modelled with flowers, leaves and elaborate scrolls. Mirror-frames were made also in the same style.

Not only was domestic and ornamental glassware developed and exported in quantity by the Venetians, but during the greater part of the sixteenth and seventeenth centuries they were the principal makers of mirror-glass and their products were far ahead of those of their imitators. It must be remembered that the making of glass in Venice has been continuous for many hundreds of years, and the same designs have been reproduced there again and again. Many sixteenth- and seventeenth-century pieces were copied in Victorian times and more recently, and the collector must guard against these copies as well as against deliberate forgeries.

England

It is probable that good glass was made in England during the Roman occupation, but when that ended little other than plain utilitarian pieces were made for a considerable time. It is known that there were glass-makers in Surrey and Sussex, where timber was plentiful, from the twelfth to the sixteenth centuries. Also, it is known that coloured glass for church windows was made at several centres.

In the sixteenth century domestic needs were supplied by glass imported principally from Venice, and some was made in the Venetian manner by Italian workers who settled in London but did not stay. In 1575 Queen Elizabeth I granted Jacopo Verzelini a privilege for twenty-one years, during which he should make Venice glasses in London and teach Englishmen the art; at the same time, importation of such glasses was prohibited by law but possibly not in fact. A number of glasses exist which it has been suggested were the work of Verzelini, but it has been impossible so far to prove this and they remain the subject of argument. A typical goblet, in the Victoria and Albert Museum, is engraved with the date 1581, and the names of 'John' and 'Jone Dier'; other rather similar pieces are dated from 1577 to 1586.

For the next seventy years a series of men held monopolies from the government for glass-making, and in the same period a change was made in substituting coal for wood in heating the furnaces. Little has been identified as having been made during this lengthy period, but it is suggested that much of the glass made then, and earlier, is so like true Venetian that it cannot now be told apart. One truly recognizable article of which the making began late in the seventeenth century is the wine-bottle. Fortunately, it was a custom in many instances to make them with the addition of a circular glass seal on the shoulder on which was the name of the owner and the date, and many of these have survived. A study of both seals and bottles has enabled a sequence of styles to be noted, and it is possible to date a bottle by its shape even when no seal is present.

It had long been considered that English glass was an inferior material, both in appearance and strength, to the imported Venetian, and in 1673 the London Glass-Sellers' Company engaged George Ravenscroft to experiment and find a substitute for 'cristallo'. The result of his researches was that the addition of a quantity of lead oxide in the form of litharge made an excellent glass that not only equalled, but even excelled, the Venetian. As powdered flints were also a part of the new composition it was given the name of 'flint glass' but it is called often nowadays 'glass-of-lead'.

Ravenscroft's first pieces suffered from a defect known as 'crisselling', in which the glass is covered in a fine crackle which clouds it. This was cured, and in 1676 it was announced that Ravenscroft had gained permission to mark his productions. The mark chosen was a small seal with the appropriate device of a raven's head in relief. Not more than a dozen sealed pieces have survived, and most of them are now in museums. Following the success of 'glass-of-lead', it was adopted throughout England. One feature of the new material was that it could not be blown quite as thinly as the Venetian, but it lent itself to the making of articles that were bright in appearance and could compare well with natural rock crystal.

The most popular production of the eighteenth century was that of wine-glasses, and thousands remain of which the different patterns defy calculation. A particularly pleasing feature of many is the 'twist' stem; these are clear, white, or coloured; the latter rarest and most expensive. The earliest glasses have a folded foot (with the outer edge turned under), later ones are with a plain thin edge.

In 1745 a duty was levied on all glass; as the duty was on the actual material the amount of this in each article was lessened, and more labour and time were expended on ornamentation. To this, together with changing fashion, is due the rise of cutting, enamelling and engraving, which played an increasing part as the century advanced. Members of the Beilby family of Newcastle-on-Tyne are famous for their enamel work. Decanters, introduced about 1750 and plain at first, became cut heavily, and before long cutting was the principal decoration of all pieces.

Chandeliers and pairs of candelabra were greatly in demand in the last half of the eighteenth century. The complex cut patterns glittered brilliantly by candlelight, enhanced by hanging chains of small glass drops. Old examples can still be bought, and most of them have been converted skilfully for use with electricity.

In Bristol, articles were made of a porcelain-like white glass, often painted delicately in colours. Blue and amethyst-coloured glass was made there also, but the majority seen today has been manufactured in recent years and probably not in England. Nearby, at Nailsea, a large factory made jugs, rolling-pins and similar domestic pieces. Many of these were in green-tinted bottle-glass, which was taxed at a lower rate and could be sold cheaply, others are made of glass striped in mixed colours. Pieces are described for convenience as 'Nailsea' and 'Bristol', but similar articles were made at glassworks up and down the country and it is rarely possible to say exactly whence they came.

Ireland

Irish glass, particularly Waterford, has been the subject of discussion for many years, but in fact it cannot usually be distinguished from that made in England at the same time. When some further Excise duties were placed on English glass in the last quarter of the eighteenth century, a few manufacturers sent craftsmen across to Ireland and opened factories there. A number of decanters have survived with raised inscriptions under the base reading 'Penrose, Waterford' and 'Cork Glass Co.', and these are indisputably of Irish make.

Germany

The hold of the Venetians on the markets of Europe was a strong one, and continual efforts were made to break it in all the countries concerned. The Germans were skilled at enamelling their glass, but it was of Venetian type and only the quality of the painting makes it noteworthy. Late in the seventeenth century they managed to develop a heavy type of crystal glass to which they applied cutting on the wheel: a revolving fine grindstone against which the article was held for pattern-making. This was a method first used in ancient times by lapidaries in the forming of gemstones, but had been employed also by the Roman glassmakers notably, as mentioned above, in the Portland Vase. The German craftsmen had already achieved success in engraving natural rock-crystal, which was then mounted elaborately in gold set with gems, and it was not a difficult step to adapt their skill to glass. The most famous of these engraving establishments were in Berlin, Petersdorf in Silesia (now Poland), and Cassel.

The fine workmanship of the earlier craftsmen was not equalled by their successors, but the glasswares of Silesia and Bohemia continued to be made throughout the eighteenth century. A milky-white glass, often decorated in enamel colours, was very popular and much of this has survived. It can be confused with the rare white Bristol product by the inexperienced, but is seen to be commonplace when compared closely. A deep red, or ruby, glass was made in the early and mid-nineteenth century, and cut in the manner of 150 years earlier. It was exported and proved highly popular in England; much of it was of clear glass 'flashed' with a thin coating of red cut through with scenes of stag-hunting and views of German spas.

Holland

Glass of Venetian type was made in the Netherlands in the seventeenth and eighteenth centuries, but it was in the decoration of glass that the Dutch excelled. Like the Germans, they ornamented much of their output with cutting on the wheel, but a speciality was engraving with a diamond which was often done so finely that the decoration can be seen only when the light falls across it. There are specimens of diamond-engraving in the Rijksmuseum, Amsterdam, dated 1600 and 1604, and similar work was done throughout the seventeenth and eighteenth centuries. The names of Frans Greenwood (a Dutchman in spite of his English surname) and David Wolff are the best known of those who did this delicate work. Some of the surviving examples are signed and dated, but many bear no indication of artist or of when they were executed. Some of the late eighteenth-century engravings were on English glasses of the period, which were then being imported into Holland.

At the end of the eighteenth century an artist named Zeuner, of whom remarkably little is known in the way of personal details, executed a number of paintings on glass. These were done in an unusual manner, with gold and silver leaf laid on the back of the glass which was then scratched through and filled with black paint. The skies in outdoor scenes were painted in natural colours, and the effect is striking and decorative. Some of his surviving works are of views in Amsterdam, and a small panel in the Victoria and Albert Museum shows a view of the Sadler's Wells Theatre, London, in about 1780.

France

The French were the most noted makers of stained glass for windows, and this was not only for their own churches but was sent abroad. Domestic glassware, as elsewhere, was of Venetian style and of no particular distinction. Nevers and Rouen had works at which were made small figures in coloured and white glasses; some of them date to as early as about 1600 but many surviving specimens are later. Most of them have little individuality with which to establish their exact provenance, as they were made also in Germany, Italy and England.

It was at the end of the eighteenth century that French glass-making began to develop, and factories were opened to make glass 'in the manner and quality of England'; whence had come much that had been imported. A factory at Baccarat, near Lunéville in 1765, was followed two years later by the Cristallerie de St Louis, in Lorraine, and others who have remained less renowned came and went. The method was invented of enclosing white ceramic medallions in clear crystal, which gave the former an attractive silver appearance; paper-weights, goblets, and other pieces were made with this type of ornamentation.

At the two factories mentioned above, and at a third in Clichy, were produced the paper-weights of clear glass decorated within with coloured 'canes' of the same material. Specimens with dates between 1845 and 1849 are found, and some are marked additionally with 'B' for Baccarat, 'C' for Clichy, and 'SL' for St Louis. It should be mentioned that the dates on such examples are never set centrally, but always to one side and even then are often scarcely noticeable. Within the last few years much attention has been paid to paper-weights from these factories, and their value has greatly appreciated. A very scarce specimen has fetched over $3,000, but less exotic ones can be purchased for a few dollars. It may be noted that they have been faked extensively. Commonplace copies with blurred coloured 'canes' inside and centrally placed dates are easily recognized, but during the last ten years some extremely clever copies of rare specimens have been made.

China

While glass was known in China from the fifth century A.D., little is known about what was made and no early specimens have been identified with certainty. A glasshouse was started under the Emperor K'ang Hsi and again there is little positive information about the productions, but a number of pieces of experimental types have been assumed to date from that time. Later, in the reigns of Yung Chêng and Ch'ien Lung (together covering the years 1723 to 1795), pieces were made of opaque tinted glass. These pieces are noticeably heavy in weight in comparison with European examples, and the colours are distinctive and pleasing. Vases were made in the shape of monochrome-glazed porcelain of the periods, and with the surface polished on the wheel. Snuff-bottles and other pieces are found imitating remarkably closely the colour and texture of jade and other hard-stones. The Chinese mastered the technique of copying onyx and other layered stones by making articles of two layers of glass, cutting through one to reveal the contrasting colour of the other. Clear glass snuff-bottles were decorated in the nineteenth century by the tedious process of painting them on the inside surface by introducing a brush through the narrow neck opening.

America

It is known that Captain John Smith sent back to England a sample of glass made on American soil in 1609, but doubtless the anonymous maker and his successors made purely utilitarian pieces. The greatest demand would be for window-glass and for bottles; a demand that continued for many years to come. Numerous glasshouses came and went during the course of the eighteenth century: Richard Wistar advertised in 1769 'between Three and Four Hundred Boxes of Window Glass . . . Lamp Glass . . . Bottles . . . Snuff and Mustard Receivers, and Retorts of various Sizes, also Electrifying Globes and Tubes, &c.', while in 1773 Henry William Steigel had for sale: 'decanters . . . tumblers . . . wine glasses . . . jelly and cillabub glasses . . . wide-mouth bottles for sweetmeats . . . phyals for doctors', etc.

As can be understood, not a great quantity of American-made glass from before 1800 has survived, and examples show divergent styles. Both English and German immigrants owned or worked in the glasshouses of the time, and each brought the skills and patterns of his homeland. Not only is it a matter of difficulty to distinguish between the productions of the various factories on American soil, but wares made in many of the lesser European factories at about the same date are not dissimilar.

Pocket spirit-flasks were in demand at the end of the eighteenth century, and usually were made by blowing the molten glass into an ornamented mould; the ornament being impressed on the article when it cooled and was removed from the hinged mould.

In the nineteenth century, once the United States had become independent, imports were discouraged and manufacturing of goods increased. Innumerable glassworks opened, but none stayed the course solely by making table or ornamental wares; profits from them were insufficient and window-glass and bottles were the mainstays. Finally, a machine for making pressed glass-ware was invented and came into use about 1828. Pressing involves the placing of molten glass into a mould, then a further mould is pressed on the still-molten material to force it into shape; one or both moulds could bear ornamentation, depending on the shape of the finished article. This provided a quick and cheap method of making imitations of cut-glass, and of introducing further ornament, for instance beading, which was not practicable on the wheel.

Pressed coloured glass was made in great quantities. The Boston and Sandwich Glassworks, of Sandwich, Mass., founded in 1828 by Deming Jarves, is probably the best-known source, but very many other factories, both large and small, made similar wares which are barely distinguishable one from another. Some examples are marked with the name of the maker, but many cannot be assigned to any particular factory.

Copies of some of the French mid-nineteenth-century glass paper-weights were made at the Boston and Sandwich Glassworks, and some original designs also were produced there.

BOOKS

The standard works on English glass are *British Table and Ornamental Glass,* by L. M. Angus-Butterworth; *From Broad Glass to Cut Crystal,* by D. R. Guttery, both books distributed in the United States by Arco Publishing Company; New York; and *A History of English and Irish Glass,* by W. A. Thorpe, 1929, in two volumes. Less comprehensive, also by W. A. Thorpe, is *English Glass.** W. B. Honey's *Glass* (Victoria and Albert Museum, 1946), deals with all countries.

CHAPTER SIXTEEN

Silver and plate

ENGLISH

SILVER IS a so-called 'noble' metal, both its appearance and its uses have earned it this title. It has been employed for many centuries for coinage, jewellery and for making useful and ornamental articles. The pure metal is too soft to withstand normal wear and tear, and therefore it has to be mixed with small proportions of others to make an alloy strong enough to retain its shape and thickness. Without complicated tests it is not possible to tell just how much actual silver is contained in any given quantity of the alloy, and a clear field is left for fraud. To safeguard the purchaser a system of testing and marking, known as 'Hall-marking' because it was first carried out at Goldsmith's Hall in London, was instituted as long ago as the year 1300.

From then onwards a number of statutes directed that silverware should be marked with a lion passant to denote it was up to sterling standard, then with a further mark indicating the maker;

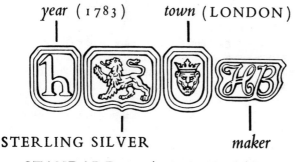

year (1783)   *town* (LONDON)

STERLING SILVER   *maker*

STANDARD   (HESTER BATEMAN)

Fig. 6. Examples of marks on a spoon, 1783.

and another, a letter of the alphabet, standing for the year in which the marking was done. Additional modifications included a figure of Britannia stamped on pieces with a higher percentage of pure silver than the normal; a mark showing the town where the assay was made: a leopard's head for London, an anchor for Birmingham, a crown for Sheffield, etc.; and the head of the sovereign from 1784 until 1890 denoting that Excise Duty on the article had been paid. The marks can be checked against published tables which are obtainable easily, and from them can be learned the exact year in which a piece was marked. It is also possible in most instances to trace the name of the maker.

Although silver is valued by weight it is offered for sale usually by the piece, and the more an article is in demand the higher is the price per ounce. It should be remembered that silversmiths use Troy weight:

> 1 pound = 12 ounces
> 1 ounce = 20 pennyweights (dwts.)
> 1 dwt. = 24 grains

Pieces of old silver often have the weight engraved on the underside. The same weights are used for gold, and the quality of the metal is given in carats; which refer to the proportion of pure gold present out of a total of twenty-four parts. Thus, the expression 18-carat gold means that a piece is made from metal composed of eighteen parts of pure gold with six of alloy; 9-carat has nine parts of gold and fifteen of alloy, and so forth.

There are severe penalties for forging marks and for selling unmarked or false silver, but occasional fakes are found. In the nineteenth century it was fashionable to take plain pieces of earlier period and ornament them with embossing and engraving. This work was sometimes accompanied by a 'slight' alteration to the piece; for instance, tankards were turned into jugs by the addition of a spout, and chamber-pots into loving-cups by soldering on an extra handle. Embellishments and alterations of these kinds affect both the appearance and the value of a piece, and it is as well for the beginner to be suspicious of anything offered at a bargain price. As with other antiques of value, a reputable dealer who understands his goods will guide the purchaser soundly.

Of the earlier pieces of silver not a great number have survived, and most of them are in churches, museums or otherwise unlikely to come on the open market. Enormous quantities were melted down during the Civil War, and the majority of old examples to be seen for sale are not older than the last quarter of the seventeenth century. Following the restoration of the monarchy, wealthy men set about replacing their possessions, and great quantities of silverware were made. Much of it was the work of refugees who had come to England recently from the Continent, whence they had fled from religious persecution. Among these Huguenot craftsmen are numbered: Paul de Lamerie, Augustine Courtauld, Pierre Harache and Simon Pantin, recognized for their high standards of workmanship.

The design of silverware was subject to many of the same influences that affected the design of other articles in the home. Turned legs on chairs are reflected in the baluster stems of candle-sticks; cabriole legs appear in miniature as supports for cream-jugs and sauce-boats; Chinese patterns were moulded or engraved on articles of all kinds, and teapots and caddies have knobs in the form of squatting Orientals; Adam husks and rams' heads were moulded or embossed, or delicately engraved; and Paul Storr, the early nineteenth-century silversmith, employed the varied fantasies of the Regency either individually or all at the same time.

Changes in domestic customs had an equally marked result. The introduction of tea and coffee drinking at the end of the seventeenth century had a big effect on silversmithing, and called forth a great variety of pieces. Early teapots were modelled on those imported of Chinese porcelain or Yi-hsing red stoneware; later silver ones, in turn, affected the shape of porcelain and pottery teapots. Cream-jugs, sugar-basins, teaspoons and caddies all came into being with the spreading popularity of the drink. Wine-labels were first used in the mid-eighteenth century, when glass decanters elegant enough for the dining-table were made.

Fish slices were known at about the same time, but the forks to accompany them did not appear until about 1800. Much can be learned of the customs of our ancestors from a study of the subject, and many of the things they used have been in continual employment since they were made.

Eighteenth-century Scottish and Irish silver has its devotees, and much is of excellent workmanship. Often it has an admirable simplicity of line, but most resembles closely the English wares of the period and it is, of course, rarer. Pieces from both of these countries were marked in a manner similar to those of England, but with letters and symbols that clearly indicate their origin.

Continental

The sale at Sothebys in London of a silver dinner service made in Paris between 1735 and 1738 focused attention on foreign silver. The 168 pieces, made by the eminent silversmith Jacques Roettier, which had been in one family since they were made, fetched $579,600 (£207,000). Such a very large sum is unusual for a single lot of silver of any nationality, but the service was a most outstanding one. The price it realized need not alarm the average collector, for the majority of foreign silver fortunately can be bought for considerably less money.

Just as English silver suffered great losses during the Civil War, so the many wars that raged on the Continent during the seventeenth and eighteenth centuries caused the destruction of large quantities almost everywhere. Further, in France, the Revolution and the Napoleonic Wars wiped out a very large proportion of the remaining early French pieces. In view of the turbulent history of every country it is surprising that any silver has survived anywhere, but in fact a considerable amount can be found. As in other branches of collecting, however, there is a shortage of pieces of the highest quality.

On the whole, the study of much Continental silver is made difficult by a lack of information on the subject; few reliable books have been published, and authoritative opinions are hard to obtain. In spite of numerous regulations enforcing both assaying and marking much old foreign silverware is unmarked, and to complicate the matter there is a glut of fakes.

The earliest pieces of any nationality are extremely rare and seldom to be seen outside the strongest showcases of the largest museums. Pieces made in the seventeenth and eighteenth centuries are sometimes to be bought, but the more important ones are expensive.

The most sought include: seventeenth-century cups of all kinds, many of German origin and often in unusual forms; Swedish tankards of large size on ball feet and each with a coin set in the cover; Dutch and German teapots in styles that were imitated closely in Continental porcelain; almost anything French of the early eighteenth century or before. However, the written word can give little idea of the masterpieces and near-masterpieces that were made in each country; the actual pieces must be seen and studied. In most instances this is achieved best in the land of their origin.

American

American silver was made first in the mid-seventeenth century, and for a considerable time after showed strong foreign influences: Dutch, French and Scandinavian clearly being discernible in many instances. Further, the earliest silversmiths were two Englishmen, John Hull and Robert Sanderson, of Boston, Massachusetts. While makers' marks are found, either in the form of initials or the full name, date letters were not used. Pieces can be dated only by their style, by the known working-period of their maker or, if there is a dated one, by an inscription. Early American silver is very rare, and most of the important surviving specimens are in museums in the major cities or in the art galleries of colleges.

Among the earlier successful Boston makers were John Allen and John Edwards, Jeremiah Dummer, Edward Winslow and John Coney. The latter took as apprentice the famous patriot and silversmith, Paul Revere (1735–1818), whose ride from Charlestown to Lexington in 1775 was immortalized with due poetic licence by Longfellow. Revere is not only an American hero, but his craftsmanship has earned him the appreciation of collectors.

New York boasted a group of Dutch makers together with others of French descent. Other centres of silver-making were Philadelphia, Connecticut, Baltimore and Annapolis in Maryland, and Newport, Rhode Island. The variety of pieces made was much smaller than that of European countries. On the whole, large pieces were either never made or have disappeared; a Baltimore soup-tureen is believed to be unique.

In view of its rarity and the zeal with which it is sought, American silver has been faked. Ingeniously, English and foreign pieces have had marks removed, leaving only one or more that might be interpreted as those of an American maker.

Sheffield Plate

The manufacture of Sheffield plate was made possible by the discovery in 1743 that plates of silver and copper could be fused together to form one indivisible sheet of metal. Thus, an article could be manufactured exactly similar in exte nal appearance to one of solid silver, but from material costing far less. The inventor of the process was a Sheffield cutler, Thomas Bolsover (1704–88).

For some years only small articles were made, but by 1760 production had increased and bigger pieces were attempted with success. Later, it was found possible to plate an ingot of copper on both sides, and it was then no longer necessary to coat the inside or underside of an article with tin; which had been done hitherto. As methods had been devised already for concealing the red line of copper showing where it was cut on an edge, the resemblance to silver was very close. The deception was aided further by the fact that some makers marked their wares with stamps that could be confused easily with those on silver.

Production of Sheffield plate received a fillip when a duty of 6d an ounce was levied on silverware in 1784, and again in 1815 when the duty was raised to 1s 6d an ounce. The ware was made in quantity between 1780 and 1830 and a surprisingly large amount has survived. After 1830 little was made, and then began the plating of silver on a base of German silver (an alloy which showed silvery when the outer coat of real silver wore through). Finally, in 1838 this was superseded by the introduction of electroplating.

Genuine Sheffield plate in good condition is scarce; in the course of time the coating of silver has often worn away in places and the copper is revealed clearly. When this happens the piece can be given a fresh coat of silver electrically, but the colour and texture of the old cannot be reproduced. Once Sheffield plate has been tampered with in this way much of its value has been lost for ever, and the careful buyer will not want to add such specimens to his collection.

BOOKS

The standard work dealing with the marks of English silversmiths as well as date-letters and hall-marks is:

English Goldsmiths and Their Marks, by Sir Charles J. Jackson. A useful and comprehensive guide to the same subject is *English Domestic Silver*, by Charles Oman*; hall-marks and date-letters are located conveniently in a clearly printed pocket-sized booklet, compiled by Frederick Bradbury of Sheffield, obtainable from most good silversmiths.*

Frederick Bradbury's *History of Old Sheffield Plate* (1902), is a standard work.

A Metropolitan Museum of New York Picture Book, *Early American Silver** is a useful illustrated introduction to the subject.

CHAPTER SEVENTEEN

Enamels

ENAMELS are types of glass, clear or opaque, used for painting on porcelain and also for decorating metals. The latter include bronze, copper, silver and gold. There are several different ways in which metals may be enamelled:

Champlevé: small spaces are scraped from, or moulded in, the surface of the article and filled with enamel. This technique was used first many centuries ago and is said to have been introduced to both the Orient and Europe from Constantinople, capital of the Byzantine empire.

Cloisonné: the body of the article is covered in a series of cells (or 'cloisons') by means of wire soldered on to the surface. The cells are filled with enamel powdered and mixed into a paste, careful firing melts the powder without disturbing the soldering, and after the enamel has been levelled and polished the metalwork is gilded. The Chinese and Japanese were very skilful workers in this technique, and Chinese pieces of the Ch'ien Lung period are not uncommon. Earlier examples are scarce.

Plique à jour: rather similar to cloisonné, but the metal wires form open windows filled with transparent enamels.

Basse Taille: the surface of the patterned metal is covered with a coating of transparent enamel through which the design can be seen. This method and the foregoing, *plique à jour*, were used principally for the decoration of jewellery and snuff-boxes.

Painted enamels: usually these are in colours on a white ground; the white being fired on a copper base before further colours are added. Grounds of colours other than white are used in a similar manner. The French at Limoges made finely painted plaques from the end of the fifteenth century onwards. Examples are rare and valuable, but they have been imitated. European enamels introduced to China in the eighteenth century inspired copies, and the Cantonese made them plentifully in the reigns of Yung Chêng and Ch ien Lung. Many of them are very well painted, some with European scenes and figures copied from engravings. It should be remembered that they have been made continuously with little variation in style, but modern pieces do not have the careful finish of the old.

One of the best-known names connected with enamels in England is that of Battersea; a factory to which a great amount of the work made elsewhere is popularly ascribed. At York House, Battersea, just outside London, enamelled copper wares were made between 1753 and 1756. Its principal claim to remembrance is that it was the seat of the first use of printing for decorating enamels; a process used shortly on porcelain. Pieces definitely made at Battersea are few, and the majority of eighteenth-century English enamels were made in the Bilston area of south Staffordshire. Contemporary Continental examples were of similar design; these and modern copies present many problems to the collector.

CHAPTER EIGHTEEN

Metalwork

Iron and Steel

Iron can be divided into two types: with little carbon content
it becomes malleable and is steel or wrought-iron, and with
more than the minimum of carbon remaining in its composition
it is cast-iron and inclined to be brittle. Probably the greatest use
of the metal in the past was in the making of armour and arms.
Armour was used both for protection in battle and in jousting,
and for ceremonial purposes. In the first instances it was designed
not only to resist blows from lances and cudgels but to deflect
them and upset the opponent's balance. Ceremonial equipment
on the other hand, displayed the art of the armourer to the best
advantage and exhibited his prowess at ornamenting a suit in
the most striking manner. Fine armour of either type is now
extremely rare outside museums, and even if it was available very
few collectors have space in which to display it adequately.
Embellishment takes the form of engraving, gilding, raised patterns, and damascening: inlay in gold and silver.

Swords and other hand weapons were often highly decorated;
early ones of fine quality are rare, but seventeenth- and eighteenth-
century examples can be found.

Firearms have received a great amount of study in the last few
years, and the value of a good pistol has risen enormously. The
subject is a very wide one and cannot be dealt with briefly.
Mechanisms for firing the charge of gunpowder and ejecting the
missile can be divided into recognizable types that make dating
possible, but only within wide limits. From the sixteenth to
seventeenth centuries the powder was ignited by means of a
wheel-lock, a hardened toothed wheel which attempted to strike
sparks from a piece of flint—comparable to a cigarette-lighter.
Its successor, introduced early in the seventeenth century, was
the *flint-lock*, in which a piece of flint gripped in steel jaws was

sprung down on to the powder and ignited it as it struck the steel powder-pan. This method endured until early in the nineteenth century, when a small cap, containing chemicals that detonated on being hit, known as a *percussion cap*, was invented. The cap was placed near the powder, and when the trigger was pressed the hammer fell and the gunpowder was exploded by the cap.

With the settlement of America there was a big demand for reliable firearms that could be made cheaply and in quantity. While all guns and pistols had been loaded from the muzzle, a practical breech-loader was invented in America in 1810. An important part in the development of firearms during the nine-teenth century was played by Samuel Colt, born at Hartford, Connecticut, in 1814. He invented, manufactured and continually improved an automatic revolver, and his name remains linked inseparably with such weapons throughout the world.

The Italians and Germans were foremost in the making and decoration of armour, and allied crafts were the making of ornamented caskets and strong-boxes with locks and keys in elaborate designs. While Continental guns were generally pre-eminent, with the development of the pistol English firearms were often as good as any others made in the eighteenth century.

Japanese armour is not greatly appreciated outside its native land, but swords and daggers are collected widely. The Japanese metalworkers were amazingly skilful in tempering and water-marking blades during manufacture, and their artistry was matched by that of the men making handles and mounts. Many of the mounts (known as Tsuba) are of iron inlaid with gold and silver in designs illustrating religious and other stories little known in Europe. The handle (Kodzuka) of the short dagger is also frequently the subject of similar decoration.

The most popular use of cast-iron was for the fireplace, where its hard-wearing qualities gave admirable service: as andirons, on which logs were supported: as firebacks to prevent the heat from damaging the building and to reflect it into the room; and in the form of grates to burn the coal which replaced wood. Much of this equipment for English homes from the fourteenth century onwards was made in Sussex, where ironworks prospered for as long as the forests of the county yielded wood for their furnaces.

In recent years attention has been given to nineteenth-century garden furniture made of iron, and for this purpose it seems admirably suited. The use of iron for furniture had several advocates in the 1830's, and many designs were published for chairs and tables in which it was used for the supports. The iron bedstead was introduced also at about that date, but did not become widely popular until twenty years later. In the words of a Victorian designer: 'where carved work, or much ornament, is to be executed in furniture, cast iron will always be found cheaper than wood'. In spite of this, the public was not convinced of its merits and little iron indoor furniture survives. In Germany, in the beginning of the nineteenth century, a method was found of casting very delicate tracery in iron, and jewellery was made from the metal. Surprisingly close imitations of bronzes were made there also from iron.

Bronze

Bronze is an alloy of copper and tin. Its use in prehistoric days is outside the scope of this book and the most important examples that will concern readers are those made in Italy and elsewhere from the sixteenth century and onwards. The making of bronze articles and figures calls for great skill. Most were made by the 'cire-perdue' (lost wax) process, which can be described briefly as follows: the piece is modelled thinly in wax on a core of dry clay, the finished wax is then covered in a coat of clay. Holes are left so that molten metal can be poured in to take the place of the wax, which is melted and runs out. The outer clay coating is broken off, the inner core chipped away, and the article finished by hand to remove any roughness or imperfections. Thus, it can be seen that each single bronze has to be modelled individually and with care, and that each version of the same original is slightly different from the others. All old bronzes were made by this method, which is still in use. The making of bronzes by means of a number of removable and re-usable small moulds, each of which leaves ridges on the article where it is joined, came into use in the nineteenth century. Traces of these ridges usually remain visible and their presence is taken generally as a certain sign of modern manufacture.

Among Italian modellers may be mentioned: Donatello, Andrea Briosco (called Riccio), Jacopo Tatti (called Sansovino) and the Flemish-born Giovanni di Bologna. German makers include the Vischer family, and the French sculptors Falconet and Clodion often had their work cast in bronze. The Frenchman Guillaume Coustou modelled the figures of rearing horses, known as the Marly Horses, about 1745. They were made in bronze, and in metals imitating bronze, in very large numbers in the nineteenth century. A number of good bronzes were made in England in the eighteenth century, but little is known yet about them.

Chinese and Japanese bronzes of great age and great size have been made for many hundreds of years. In addition to figures there are some fifteenth-century bells at Pekin weighing about fifty-five tons each and standing fourteen feet high. Chinese bronze altar-vessels of the Shang-Yin (1766–1122 B.C.) and Chou dynasties (1122–249 B.C.) are particularly fine and rare. Most have been buried for many centuries, and contact with earth has resulted in corrosion of the surface. Inevitably, these bronzes have been copied at later dates, but the true patina (ageing of the surface) presents a very difficult problem to the faker and it is one that is seldom solved with success.

Mention must be made of the very many fine bronze figures made in India and Siam (Thailand) in the sixteenth century A.D. and earlier. Some of the latter are gilt, and most are remarkably beautiful. The finer examples remain in the East or are in Western museums, but a few appear on the market from time to time. Reasonably good examples can sometimes be bought quite cheaply.

In west Africa, the skilful bronze and brass workers of the kingdom of Benin perhaps learned their craft from the Portuguese, with whom they had traded from the late fifteenth century. Their work is highly individual and much is very beautiful, but it is scarce and good specimens are obtainable only rarely. Examples were brought to Europe by a British punitive expedition which captured Benin city in 1897, and there are fine collections from this source at the British Museum, the Pitt-Rivers Museum, Farnham, Dorset, the Museum of Primitive Art, New York, and in the possession of the Government of Nigeria.

Brass

The most popular surviving form of brassware is probably the domestic candlestick. These were made usually in pairs, and are rarely older than the middle of the seventeenth century. At that time they were on domed circular bases, with a pan to catch drips of wax halfway up the stout central column. Early in the eighteenth century, shaped bases and tall stems with grease-pans at the very top came into fashion. With variations from time to time, this style continued in use until the candle was no longer the principal illuminant in the home.

Fig. 7. Brass candlesticks, *l. to r.:* 1720, 1650, 1760.

Brass was made into dishes of various sizes, often with embossed designs of Biblical scenes with inscriptions on the borders. These are sometimes still to be seen in use as alms-dishes in churches.

Chandeliers of brass with curved branching arms were made in England and also on the Continent. Many of them date from the seventeenth century, but most have been made more recently in response to continual demand.

Ormolu

This is the French name (literally *or moulu*, moulded gold) for articles and furniture mounts made of bronze and gilded. The piece having been made in bronze, was carefully and finely finished by chiselling and polishing and then coated with a mixture of mercury and gold. This amalgam was subjected to heat and the mercury evaporated leaving the gold deposited on the surface. Finally, the gold was burnished where required, or left matt.

The French developed the art of designing and making furniture mounts from ormolu, and were equally proficient at making clockcases, candlesticks, inkstands and other suitable pieces from the same material. Much thought was given to the mounting of porcelain in ormolu, and vases and figures with bases and other enhancements were valued highly for decoration. They fetch high prices today, but only if the mounts are genuinely of the eighteenth century. From 1745 to 1749 a tax was levied on ormolu, and pieces were stamped in a similar manner to silver. The mark is a letter 'c' beneath a crown, but as it was in use apparently for no more than four years specimens bearing it are rare.

German ormolu is not dissimilar to French, although seldom as highly finished. In England, the firm of Boulton and Fothergill, of Soho, Birmingham, made good ormolu at the end of the eighteenth century.

Old ormolu is sometimes found with the gilding in good condition, but frequently it is worn away on the surfaces exposed to wear. In the past more has been ruined by careless handling than by wear and tear; its greatest enemy is metal-polish, which should never be used on it. As with Sheffield plate, ormolu can be replated electrically but the appearance of the old cannot be reproduced exactly.

Pewter

Pewter is an alloy of tin with small additions of lead and other metals. Although it was in use for many centuries, and was displaced finally by pottery and porcelain, little remains that is earlier than the seventeenth century. It is a soft metal and subject to corrosion from the atmosphere, and it is perhaps remarkable that so much that is old has survived. The making and working of the metal was regulated by the Pewterers' Company of London from the mid-fourteenth century, and their rules stated that a worker should provide himself with a personal mark to be stamped on his wares. This mark or 'touch' was struck on a touch-plate belonging to the Company, but in 1666 the Great Fire of London destroyed the Pewterers' Hall and all its contents. The system was recommenced in 1668 and continued until the early years of the nineteenth century. At Edinburgh and in other places, a similar method was used.

In addition to the official 'touch' of the maker, many men added extra marks which were completely unofficial and bore a strong likeness to the hall-marks on silver. This resemblance was no more than superficial, and it is to be regretted that date-letters were not used on the metal.

Pewter was used for the making of domestic articles for every-day use; candlesticks, jugs, plates and dishes, tankards, spoons, and so forth. Most English pewter is devoid of decoration and relies on its good plain shaping for effect. Occasionally ornament in the form of engraving is found.

Continental pewter, on the other hand, frequently has decor-ated knobs and handles in the form of cast figures, and is often engraved.

Paktong

This is an alloy of copper, nickel and zinc, which resembles silver; it is slow to tarnish, wears well and was used occasionally in the eighteenth century for making candlesticks, fenders, grates and other articles. Paktong was imported into England from China, whence came also a pure zinc known as Tutenag. The two were often confused by writers.

BOOKS

There is no single volume dealing with the vast subject of metalwork in general, but the following books are on separate aspects:

Iron and Steel: *Handbook of Ironwork*, by J. Starkie Gardner, Victoria and Albert Museum; *Iron and Brass Implements of the English House*, by Seymour Lindsay (1927).

Bronze: *Italian Bronze Statuettes*, by W. Bode, in three volumes, published in 1907–8 is the standard work. The Wallace Collection Catalogue; *Sculpture*, by J. G. Mann (1931)* describes and illustrates many examples.

Brass: *Dinanderie*, by J. Tavenor-Perry (1910) deals with the brassware made in and about the Belgian town of Dinant in the late Middle Ages.

Ormolu: There is no book that deals exclusively with this, but the Wallace Collection Catalogue, *French Furniture*, By F. J. B. Watson (1956),* describes and illustrates many examples.

Pewter: *Old Pewter, its Makers and Marks*, by Howard H. Cotterell (1929) is the standard work. A useful introduction is *Old British Pewter*, 1500–1800, by A. V. Sutherland-Graeme; a Victoria and Albert Museum 'Small Picture Book', *British Pewter* (1960)* illustrates and describes typical examples.

Paktong: Information on this metal is in *Tutenag and Paktong*, by A. Bonnin, published at Oxford in 1924.

Part IV

MISCELLANEOUS

CHAPTER NINETEEN

Jade and other stones

STONES from comparatively hard jade to the aptly named soapstone have always presented a challenge to the craftsman. Whenever they were to be found in suitable size and shape it was an invitation to the lapidary to attempt to fashion them into works of art. The comparison between a rough natural stone and the result of careful carving and polishing never ceases to surprise and delight the onlooker. The finest specimens barely indicate the skill and patience that contributed to their finished form, but a brief study will show why the Chinese and others revered jade and why Europeans attempted to rival rock-crystal with glass.

Jade

The Oriental mind has woven a wealth of legend into this stone, which varies in colour from pale grey-green and light lavender to a deep green that is almost black in some lights. It is divided by geologists into two distinct types: jadeite and nephrite. The latter is slightly less hard and under a microscope it will be seen that 'in cross-section the fibres have cleavage cracks intersecting, not at approximately 90°, as in jadeite, but at 120°, and there are numerous other differences . . .' However, few, if any, collectors attempt to distinguish between the two, and describe them both as jade.

The stone is alleged by the Chinese to have been forged from a rainbow in order to make thunderbolts for the God of Storms,

138

and it is also the traditional, although surely unpalatable, food of the Taoist genii. By most of the nations of antiquity it was regarded as possessing magical and curative properties; not only was it looked on also as a symbol of virtue, but it was supposed to be of value in the cure of diseases affecting the kidney.

Ancient jade objects of various shapes were used for ceremonial purposes and many of them have been excavated in modern times. They have received much attention from scholars and are rarely to be seen outside museums. The Chinese jade that is most likely to be found by the collector is seldom older than the eighteenth century. Being a hard stone it acquires few signs of wear, and with the Chinese habit of copying the designs of earlier days it is not easy to determine the age of many specimens. Large pieces of undoubted age can be very costly, but small examples of less certain vintage may be found for no more than a few pounds apiece.

The so-called 'Mogul' jade is usually of a pale grey-green colour, carved very thinly and often with pierced decoration. Some was inlaid with gold and precious stones, which seem to acquire an added fire against the background of the limpid stone. The Mogul jades were made in India, but were esteemed sufficiently by the Chinese for the Imperial workshops to have a department where work in this manner was produced.

A green nephrite found in New Zealand was used by the natives to make axe-heads and ornaments. Of the latter, the 'Tiki', a ferocious-looking distorted human figure, represents the Maori Creator who 'took red clay, and kneaded it with his own blood'. These pendant talismen are flatly rendered, and usually about three inches high and one and a half inches wide. Specimens some nine inches in height are known but are very rare when so large, and collectors should beware of modern copies of them in all sizes.

Soapstone

After jade, the principal stone carved by the Chinese is soapstone, a very soft material varying in colour from a light brown or pale green to a distinctive rich and deep red. It is easily scratched with a pin and reduces to a white powder, it breaks without much difficulty, and in spite of these obvious differences is sometimes mis-called jade by optimistic owners of specimens. In the eighteenth century it was often carved in the form of figures of the Immortals of the Taoist religion; more recently it has been used for vases with carved and pierced ornament, and for wine- and tea-pots.

Old pieces of soapstone will be found to have been neatly and carefully finished, and to have a high polish that is lacking in modern specimens. Many old examples have a subtlety of colour that is worthy of a more durable material.

Quartz

A pale pink-coloured or a green-coloured variety of quartz was carved by the Chinese into decorative vases and figures. Most examples are clumsy in appearance and not very carefully carved; few are very old.

Other stones

Many other decorative stones, both large and small, have been used by lapidaries in both East and West; the list of them is too long and their descriptions too involved to be included here. However, mention must be made of two of the more important.

Derbyshire Spar, known also as Blue John (surmised to be a corruption of the French 'bleu-jaune' from the prevalent colours of the stone), an unusually vividly marked variety of fluorspar mined in Derbyshire, and made into vases and other ornaments from about 1770. Some of the finer eighteenth-century examples have ormolu mounts which were made by Matthew Boulton in Birmingham.

A transparent variety of quartz is **rock-crystal,** which was carved with consummate skill in both Classical and Renaissance times. Examples of European work are seldom seen outside the principal museums, and the magnificence of most of the surviving specimens is a clear indication of why they were, and are still, so highly valued.

Specimens of Chinese carved rock-crystal are sometimes to be seen. They take similar forms to jade, and both vases and figures were made.

Hardstones of many kinds were used for the making of decorative panels, known as Pietre Dure or Florentine Mosaics, for table-tops and other purposes by the Italians. A workshop for this purpose was started by the Grand Duke of Tuscany at the end of the sixteenth century and, apart from specimens in museums and collections all over the world, there is a museum in Florence devoted to the art (the Museo dell' Opficio delle Pietre Dure). In addition to making panels to form pictures in the manner of marquetry, but using coloured marbles and stones instead of wood, other panels were made with the inset stones carved in relief: bunches of highly polished cherries were a popular subject.

The Japanese family of Shibayama introduced the inlaying of coloured shell and other material into their ivory carvings, and from this spread the inlaying of hardstones, mother-of-pearl and anything else considered suitable into panels of lacquer. All this inlaid work is known as Shibayama, although it only faintly resembles the original work of the family.

BOOKS

Jade is the subject of *Chinese Jade Throughout the Ages*, by S. C. Nott (1936); in which pieces are described and illustrated in black and white and in colour. *Chinese Jade Carving* by S. Howard Hansford, 1950, illustrates fewer examples, but the information it contains is valuable.

CHAPTER TWENTY

Ivory

I VORY has been used for making works of art from Biblical times onwards. The comparative ease with which it can be manipulated and its durable nature have always attracted craftsmen of all nations, and the latter quality has led to the preservation of a surprisingly large number of ancient examples. While the principal pieces made prior to the seventeenth century are now in museums, occasional examples appear on the market and fetch high prices. They are usually pieces with religious significance: leaves of small folding altar-pieces (diptyches) carved finely with scenes from the life of Christ or with the history of a saint.

More within the reach of the collector are figures. If European they date mostly from the mid-seventeenth century, but are later when Oriental. German carvers were prolific workers, and their output was rivalled only by that of Flanders where the sculptor François Duquesnoy (known as Il Fiammingo) influenced many craftsmen. J. C. L. Lück made figures in ivory and also modelled in porcelain for the Meissen and other factories, and a number of porcelain groups and figures owe their origin to him and his fellow craftsmen in ivory. The range of articles made from ivory is very wide: large tankards heavily carved with numerous mythological figures and set off with elaborate silver mounts, snuff-boxes, tobacco-rasps for grating the 'noxious weed' to make snuff, candlesticks, and both religious and secular figures and groups, to name only a few.

Both the Chinese and Japanese were skilful carvers of ivory, and the former had two main centres of production: Pekin and Canton. At the latter were made many of the pieces which have been described as being 'more distinguished for bizarre complexity of pattern than for artistic feeling'. To that category belong the familiar 'concentric balls'; those ingenious collections of balls, loosely one inside the other and all of them painstakingly carved and pierced from a single piece of ivory.

142

The carvings made by the Japanese are well known for their meticulous detail, often carried to extremes. They vary in size from several inches in height to the miniature *netsuke*. The latter were used ceremonially to hold the *inro* (or small medicine box) suspended from the girdle of the kimono by a silk cord, and their design is infinitely varied. The finest are the work of men who specialized in making them and the ingenuity of their design is matched by an exquisite finish.

During the past hundred years many reproductions of European ivories of all periods have been made, and it is true to say that a large number of the pieces thought to be antique (and shown as such with pride in the cabinets of collectors) are no more than a century or so old. Equally, but in more recent years, netsuke have been copied in great numbers, not only in ivory and similar materials that resemble it, but also in such entirely worthless substances as celluloid. The modern imitations of both Eastern and Western work show few signs of the great care and skill used in making the original pieces. Further, they have usually been smeared copiously with brown stain and dirt to simulate the dust of ages and hide their casual execution.

Other animal and vegetable substances

These include a number that resemble ivory more or less closely: the teeth of the hippopotamus, walrus, narwhal, and sperm-whale, and the bones of animals. From the latter, Napoleonic prisoners of war held captive in England constructed models of sailing ships. Many of them were extremely well made, especially when the conditions in which the craftsmen lived and the lack of suitable tools and materials are considered. Models of guillotines were made also by the same men, but these are understandably less popular with collectors.

The horn of the rhinoceros was esteemed by the Chinese for use in preparing medicines and also, when in the form of a drinking-vessel, for the testing of liquids. If poison was present it was said that a white liquid would become visible. Be that as it may, the Chinese craftsmen skilfully carved cups from the brown horn, which acquires an attractive dull sheen with age, and made elaborate blackwood stands to bear them.

Tortoiseshell was known and valued by the Romans, and in more modern times was much used as a veneer on furniture in combination with brass; a type of ornamentation perfected by the French cabinet-maker A. C. Boulle at the end of the seventeenth century. During the nineteenth century, tortoiseshell was often used for veneering small articles, pin-boxes and tea-caddies being particularly favoured. Like horn, it was moulded and carved both in Europe and the Far East, and it has been imitated with varying success in celluloid and other transparent materials.

Mother-of-pearl is the lustrous pearl-like inner lining of many seashells. It is found all over the world, but shells from tropical waters are esteemed because of their large size. Complete shells were carved with religious and other scenes, tea-caddies were covered with the material, and the Chinese made many thousands of gambling counters from it. These were of various shapes and each was carefully engraved. Mother-of-pearl was employed as an inlay from the seventeenth century, both in wood and lacquer, and in Victorian times was inset in black japanned and gilt furniture, tea trays and other objects. An unusual technique was to inset minute pieces of it, carefully arranged in a pattern, into black lacquer covering a vase or a bowl of Chinese porcelain. This was done in the Far East in the eighteenth century, and such decoration is termed 'lac burgauté'.

BOOKS

English ivory-carvings are the subject of *English Ivories* by M. H. Longhurst (1926), and there are other works in foreign languages dealing with the work of Continental craftsmen. Japanese netsuke are described and illustrated in *Netsuke*, by A. Brockhaus, written in German and published in Leipzig in 1905, and *The Art of the Netsuke Carver*, by F. Meinertzhagen, London, 1956.

CHAPTER TWENTY-ONE

Clocks, watches, musical boxes

IN the first instance clocks were made to be placed prominently in outdoor positions to tell the time to the people at large. In due course, smaller examples were made for use in the home, and eventually a further reduction in size led to the introduction of the personal pocket-watch.

The earliest clocks with movements driven by the power from a falling weight had neither hands nor dial, and marked the hours by striking a bell. Eventually, a face to show the hours was added, and at a later date the hours were divided into minutes and a further hand affixed to indicate them. These clocks were heavy iron-framed affairs, usually placed high inside a tower within which the weight had a good distance to travel before it needed rewinding.

Regulation to prevent the weight crashing down from top to bottom of the tower was achieved by a device known as a *Foliot balance*. In this, the final wheel in the train was set on a horizontal spindle. The wheel, called the *crown wheel* because of its appearance, was cut with comparatively long angled teeth into which fitted alternately two flat plates (or *pallets*) on an upright spindle. At the top of this latter spindle was a shaped arm with adjustable weights at either end for regulating the speed of the clock. For smaller indoor clocks the swinging arm was replaced by a wheel, and the speed was controlled by making the weight lighter or heavier.

Early in the sixteenth century appeared the first clocks using a coiled spring instead of a weight. The fact that the power exerted by a spring grows less as it uncoils was the subject of much research, and a device known as the *fusee* was the successful outcome. It takes the form of a cone-shaped drum with grooves on to which the gut or chain from the mainspring drum is wound. As the spring is uncoiled it reaches the larger circumference and this equalizes the weakened pull. The use of springs and fusees encouraged the making of portable clocks and these, first made in Germany, soon became popular. Their time-keeping, like

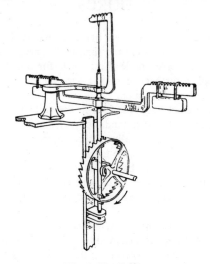

Fig. 8. The Foliot.

that of all other clocks, was erratic and the sundial remained an essential standby.

The Italian astronomer, Galileo, discovered the important property of the pendulum, but its application to clockmaking was due to a Dutchman, Christiaan Huygens. By November 1658 Johannes Fromanteel, a clockmaker of Dutch origin who lived and worked in London, was advertising that he had for sale 'Clocks that go exact and keep equaller time than any now made without this Regulater'. This was a true statement, but throughout the eighteenth century improvements of one kind and another led to greater accuracy and reliability. The names of Tompion,

Graham, Quare, and many others attained a well-deserved fame, and specimens of their workmanship are sought eagerly today.

Extremely accurate time-keeping would make it possible for a ship to find its exact position at sea, and the government offered

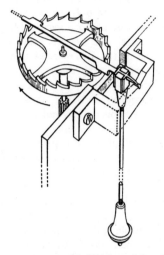

Fig. 9. Verge escapement with 'bob' pendulum in use from about 1658.

big rewards for this purpose. Harrison, Mudge and Arnold are the three most famous names in this connexion, and their pains-taking labours did much to ensure the supremacy of British shipping and the world-wide fame of British clock-making.

The earliest clocks were almost certainly made by blacksmiths; they had heavy iron frames and they show few signs of the small-scale precision associated with the work of a true clockmaker. With the advent of the portable clock came the widespread use of brass, and the accuracy and neatness typical of such mechanisms. By the middle of the eighteenth century few households were with-out a clock of some type; usually a long-case or *grandfather*.

The demand for these grew so great that the trade became divided into a number of specialists, each of whom made one or more parts. A country clockmaker ordered his requirements, assembled them and added his name on the front of the face. The majority of surviving clocks made in country towns and villages were put together in this manner, and only occasionally were they made entirely by the men whose names appear boldly on them.

The first clock cases were of gilt metal or brass, and the familiar type known as the *lantern clock* is a typical example. Wooden cases were introduced in the seventeenth century, mostly of oak veneered with ebony but later with walnut and other woods. Inlays of floral marquetry and later of satinwood and ebony stringings followed fashions that prevailed at the times of manufacture.

Whereas a good Tompion will realize a thousand pounds or more, clocks by less exalted makers can be bought comparatively cheaply. An important factor is the condition of the movement; of greater interest to the collector than the case. Continual use during the centuries will have caused wear and necessitated replacement of parts; if this has not been done with great care and by a knowledgeable craftsman much of the value will have been lost, and it will be found that it is a very expensive matter to correct it. An apparently fine clock will sometimes disclose on examination that the entire striking mechanism has been removed, or that the old escapement has been changed for a more modern, but less capricious, one. Further, movements have been adapted to fit cases, and vice versa; a long-case of small size, known as a *grandmother*, should be treated with great caution. Old examples do exist but are very rare, and the majority of them have been manufactured by unscrupulous fakers.

In France, clocks were placed in large and ornamental cases, sometimes with matching wall-brackets, covered in tortoiseshell inlaid with brass (Boulle work). The fashion lasted from about 1690, through the eighteenth century and later. In the early 1700's cases began to be veneered with kingwood, tulipwood, and other rare woods, mounted in ormolu and designed in styles to match those prevailing for furniture. Other clocks were given cases of ormolu and bronze, sometimes set with Dresden and other china groups and with Sèvres porcelain flowers. Genuine specimens are rare and expensive, and they have been copied carefully and often. A feature of an old French clock movement is that the pendulum is suspended on a silk thread, which can be lengthened or shortened to regulate the time.

German clocks often resemble closely the French. Others had movements of which the framing was of wood instead of the usual brass.

Watches

The making of pocket-watches may be said to have begun with small ones of spherical shape about 1520. These resembled pomanders and were worn similarly; from a chain round the neck, or at the girdle. The round flat watch came later, and was enclosed in a plain inner case, usually of silver, and an outer case with elaborate ornamentation. The movements are found to be most carefully made, and the *cock*, or cover of the balance-wheel, usually pierced and engraved in a complicated pattern.

The maximum decoration was given to watches by the French and Swiss: cases of gold were enamelled or set with precious stones, and intricate movements with small automata that struck the hours were made. The watches of Abraham Louis Breguet, born in Switzerland and working in France, are among the very finest ever made. He died in 1823 and it has been said by an expert that 'all his watches show perfect workmanship, originality in design and beauty in form'. Like the early eighteenth-century work of Thomas Tompion, that of Breguet has been faked, and the fame of both makers was so great in their lifetimes that many of the forgeries were contemporary with them.

Musical boxes

Musical boxes are nearly as old as clocks. They operate by a barrel with protruding pegs striking the teeth of a steel comb or operating bells. The most familiar ones are those of small size, frequently in the form of snuff-boxes, many of which are adapted to play more than one tune. They are supposed to have been invented by a Swiss, Louis Favre of Geneva, and most of the good movements were made in that country. Some are incredibly small and were fitted into fob seals, sealing-wax holders, penknives and other articles where they might surprise a listener. A refinement was the fitting of a tiny bellows to work a whistle, which led to the making of boxes containing a small hidden bird. This would pop up and sing, to disappear when the song was ended and stay hidden until the operating button was pressed again. Late in the eighteenth century clocks were fitted sometimes with a musical box in the base, which played when the hour had struck. Grandfather clocks were made to play a short tune on bells at the hour, and on some it was possible to choose one of several melodies.

In the nineteenth century many large musical boxes were made, some playing a number of tunes and fitted with interchangeable barrels. Others played principally on a steel comb, but had bells as well and incorporated small drums played by coloured butterflies. They were replaced finally by the gramophone.

BOOKS

Clocks: *Watchmakers and Clockmakers of the World*, by G. H. Baillie* (1947), lists about 35,000 names of clock and watch makers up to 1825. *Old Clocks and Watches and Their Makers*, by F. W. Britten, is the standard work. *Some Outstanding Clocks Over Seven Hundred Years — 1250-1950*, by H. Alan Lloyd, is a magnificently illustrated work on the subject; it is distributed by Arco Publishing Co., New York. Many books on the subject are published every year.

Watches: *Watches*, by G. H. Baillie (1929) and *The Story of Watches*, by T. P. Camerer Cuss. *English Watches*, by J. F. Hayward, V. & A. museum, 1956.*

Musical Boxes, and Automata: *Les Automates*, by A. Chapuis and Edmond Droz, published in Neuchâtel in 1949 and *Musical Boxes*, by J. E. T. Clark.

CHAPTER TWENTY-TWO

Embroidery, lace, tapestry

Embroidery

Although the art of embroidery was practised very many centuries ago, the collector is unlikely to be able to acquire much that was made prior to about 1650. Pieces of earlier date are extremely rare; not only are the majority of them preserved carefully in cathedrals, churches and museums, but understandably time has taken its toll.

English work of the Middle Ages was famous throughout Europe, and the remaining examples show how justly its admiration was earned. The work most likely to attract the collector is the type that was popular in the mid-seventeenth century, and known for no explicable reason as *stumpwork*. It consists of embroidery on a panel of silk (usually white) in coloured silks with some of the principal features padded out, and often having human figures with carved wood heads, hands and feet. This type of work was made in the form of pictures, for covering the frames of mirrors, and for covering boxes; the latter usually fitted with numerous small drawers (some of them 'secret'), a mirror, and lined with pink paper bordered with silver tape.

Straightforward *tent-stitch* embroidery worked on a canvas backing, dating from the seventeenth century onwards, was stitched in both wool and silk, and occasionally with threads of gold and silver. Much of it has been preserved during the past 250 years, and a proportion retains much of its original brilliant colouring. By reason of its attractive appearance and its durability it is not surprising that this type of work continues to be done today. Eighteenth-century furniture with its original (or contemporary) hand-worked covering is, of course, rare, but the value of a piece is increased greatly by its presence.

In the third quarter of the eighteenth century there was a vogue for pictures, square, oblong, round and oval, worked in coloured silks on a silk background; the latter often embellished with touches of water-colour. Most of these have faded, others are found to have backgrounds rotted with age and neglect, but perfect examples may sometimes be found and are very decorative. Subjects varied from imitations of the patterns on Chinese porcelain to renderings of willowy ladies weeping at the tomb of Shakespeare, or at that of Werther following the publication of Goethe's *Sorrows of Werther* in 1774. A lady named Mary Linwood of Leicester, achieved fame towards the end of the eighteenth century by working elaborate embroidery pictures, mostly imitating well-known paintings, sixty-four of which she exhibited in London for many years.

The familiar *sampler* began as a reference panel of patterns and stitches, but by the eighteenth century it had become an exercise for children. They were embroidered with the letters of the alphabet, mottoes, verses, texts, and the date of execution together with the name of the worker. Late in the century the making of maps became popular. These were drawn in outline on silk, and the whole, including county boundaries and names, then stitched carefully in appropriate colours.

In the nineteenth century there was a fashion for working brilliantly coloured pictures in wool; many were after famous paintings, but the greater number were of Biblical subjects. They are known as *Berlin woolwork*, for both patterns and materials were prepared and exported from Prussia. They were sewn with thick wool and in big stitches, many were of large size and must have taken a considerable time to finish.

Beadwork is allied to embroidery, and was used on its own as well as in conjunction with work in wool and silk. It was widely popular in the seventeenth century, and revived during the reign of Queen Victoria when it was used often for making banners for firescreens and panels for covering footstools.

In other parts of Europe styles similar to those of England were followed, but with local variations in both designs and materials. Similarly, in America the inhabitants followed the styles that they, or their forbears, had followed before they reached that land. Much of the work is indistinguishable from European, but samplers exist with names of individuals and cities that make their identification certain.

Chinese embroiderers favoured silk, which they had in the first place introduced into the West, of which the production was pursued with zeal. Fine embroidery was used on robes, in many instances on both sides of the fabric with the thread-ends care-

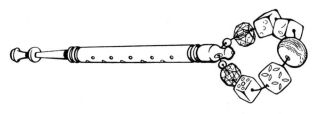

Fig. 10. Pillow lace bobbin, made of bone with coloured glass beads.
(Overall length: 4½ inches.)

fully concealed. It was used also with great effect in the form of pictures. Similar work was done by the Japanese.

Lace

Lace was once studied eagerly and extensively, but today only comparatively few collectors take notice of it. There is probably more interest shown in the equipment used in its making (pillow-lace bobbins, in particular) than in the finished material. A brief mention is made of some of the many varieties, but only the barest outline is attempted; the names of the many patterns and the stitches employed would alone fill a book.

Hand-made lace is divided into two distinct types: that made with the needle, known as *needlepoint*; and that made with bobbins on a cushion, known as *pillow*. Basically, needlepoint lace is made from one single continuous thread, and pillow-lace from a number. In the latter, each thread is wound conveniently on a bobbin made of wood or bone, often the subject of 'folk' decoration, and many are hung at one end with a bunch of coloured glass beads.

In the sixteenth century lace-making was a flourishing art, pattern books began to appear, and both Venice and Flanders were early seats of activity. Stimulus was provided by fashion decreeing that lace should be worn by both sexes, and contemporary paintings prove its popularity.

The most renowned needlepoint laces were made at Alençon and Argentan, and at Brussels. It is stated that the net forming the background in some of the finer Alençon pieces was composed of hexagons with sides one-tenth of an inch long, these sides being 'overcast with some nine or ten buttonhole stitches'.

Pillow lace was made also in Venice and Flanders, and in other countries. In England, imports from Europe threatened the native industry, and prohibition of foreign work was followed by the immigration of some of the workers themselves. English pillow lace was produced in several places, Honiton in Devonshire being the most famous. Other centres of lesser importance were: Buckinghamshire, Bedfordshire, Northamptonshire, Wiltshire, Dorset and Suffolk. Lace was made also in Ireland, principally in the nineteenth century.

Tapestry

Tapestry was used as a wall covering and, unlike needlework, was woven on a loom. Also, it was made in much larger sizes than would normally be worked in hand-stitched embroidery; panels of tapestry ten or twelve feet in height and twenty feet long are not uncommon. Wool was the material employed principally, but for special purposes silk was used. Gold and silver threads appear in many of the finest examples.

Brussels was the principal centre of tapestry-weaving from about the year 1500, and the enormous output over the years varied greatly in quality. Subjects included Roman and Biblical history, mythology, and peasant scenes after Teniers. Seventeenth- and eighteenth-century examples are often marred by the fact that time has faded their red dyes to a murky brown. Many Brussels tapestries bear a mark: a shield with a capital B at either side, and individual weavers sometimes added their names or initials.

In France there were two important factories: Beauvais and Gobelins, both founded in the second half of the seventeenth century. The former was a private concern with State support, the latter was a Royal factory and not until late in the eighteenth century could any of its productions be purchased. Both did work of high quality, Beauvais being especially famous for a series of panels based on the *Fables* of La Fontaine, and for many sets of chair and settee covers. The latter were made also at Gobelins, where in about 1775 they made some noteworthy sets of matching wall hangings and furniture covers. A superb example of this decorative harmony, in a room designed by Robert Adam, remains at Osterley Park, near London, and a suite of furniture (parted from its wall-hangings but still with its Gobelins covers) made for Moor Park in Hertfordshire, is now in the Philadelphia Museum of Art. A few more of these rich ensembles are still intact, but a set of tapestries made for a salon at Croome Park in Warwickshire was sold some years ago for the sum of £50,000, and is now in the Metropolitan Museum of Art, New York.

At Aubusson, also in France, tapestry panels, chair covers and also tapestry carpets were made. Much of the output dates from the nineteenth century, although it is similar in pattern to work of an earlier period.

Tapestry was woven in Antwerp by Michael and Philip Wauters, who specialized in supplying foreign markets. Many of the panels made popular by other factories were copied with success, and these Flemish tapestries are confused frequently with the English productions they imitate.

It can be assumed that tapestry was woven in England from an early date; a Royal decree of 1364 refers to the corporation of Tapissers, but nothing of their work has been identified. The earliest surviving pieces, positively of English make, bear dates between about 1580 and 1600 and were made on looms set up at Barcheston, Warwickshire, by William Sheldon. Some fragments of tapestry maps of English counties, and other panels, have survived, and prove that Sheldon sponsored excellent work. More important was the factory started at Mortlake in 1620.

This was under the patronage of Charles I (both as Prince of Wales and as King), and operated successfully until the Civil War, which inevitably caused a decline in orders. After 1670 little work was done at Mortlake, and the factory removed eventually to Soho, London, where production was continued throughout the first half of the eighteenth century. Although the later work was not of the outstanding quality of the earlier Mortlake tapestry, it was adequate for normal usage in both town and country.

Tapestry is subject to damage by that enemy of all woollen fabrics: the moth. In addition, its very size and weight lead to deterioration over the years, and the action of sun, damp air and heat and smoke from fires tends to perish the ageing fabric. Repair is feasible, but is apt to be expensive as there is a declining number of experts to whom such work can be entrusted.

Almost all tapestries left the loom complete with a border, varying in pattern from factory to factory and over the years, after the manner of a picture frame. In the course of time, these borders have often been mutilated or replaced, and it should be borne in mind by the collector that the presence or absence of the original border greatly affects the value of a panel.

BOOKS

Needlework: *Domestic Needlework*, by S. G. Seligman and T. Hughes illustrates and describes specimens ranging from caps and gloves to cushions and pictures. *Catalogue of English Domestic Embroidery*, by J. L. Nevinson (1950),* issued by the Victoria and Albert Museum, London.

Lace: *The Romance of Lace*, by M. E. Jones (1951) deals with the history of the subject from the Middle Ages to the nineteenth century.

Tapestry: *A History of Tapestry*, by W. G. Thomson (1930), *French Tapestry*, by Andre Lejard (1946), and *English Tapestries of the 18th Century*, by H. C. Marillier (1930).

Index